# THE ASYLUM OF DR. CALIGARI

atch out for James Morrow:
He's magic."
*Vashington Post Book World*

WORLD FANTASY AWARD WINNER

**JAMES MORROW**

## ADVANCE PRAISE FOR *TH*

"No one does history-meet *Asylum of Dr. Caligari* is a great example—impressionism versus expressionism, psychology in the asylum of 'dreams,' the weaponization of art, big laughs and big ideas, a wild imagination, and smooth, subtle writing."
—Jeffrey Ford, author of *A Natural History of Hell*

"*The Asylum of Dr. Caligari* is a fast, funny book . . . Brilliantly walking the line, its zippy energy camouflages a surprisingly powerful resonance. It's yet another seriocomic triumph from one of the genre's best satirists."
—Christopher East

"I was reminded time and again of some horror greats, including *Dracula* and *Frankenstein*."
—*The Booklover's Boudoir*

"One of the joys of *The Asylum of Dr. Caligari* is its portrayal of the intellectual ferment of the first two decades of the twentieth century. Discussions of the value of the new science of psychology, of non-expressionistic art forms, of philosophers such as Nietzsche, and of the evolution of warfare are strewn throughout the story."
—*Amazing Stories*



## PRAISE FOR JAMES MORROW

"Morrow is the only author who comes close to Vonnegut's caliber."
—*The Stranger*

"The most provocative satiric voice in science fiction."
—*Washington Post*

"I am so besotted with James Morrow's talent that I cannot find a word big enough to deify it."
—Harlan Ellison, bestselling author of *Shatterday*

"Christianity's Salman Rushdie, only funnier and more sacrilegious."
—*Denver Post*

"Widely regarded as the foremost satirist associated with the SF and Fantasy field."
—*SF Site*

**ON THE *MADONNA AND THE STARSHIP***

[STAR] "Jonathan Swift meets Buck Rogers in this hilarious send-up of the golden ages of television and pulp sci-fi."
—*Publishers Weekly*, starred review

"*Galaxy Quest*, eat your heart out."
—*Bookish*

"A work of wit and substance."
—*New York Review of Science Fiction*

**ON *SHAMBLING TOWARDS HIROSHIMA***

"Sharp-edged, delightfully batty . . . skillfully mingling real and imaginary characters with genuinely hilarious moments."
—*Kirkus*

"Witty, playful . . . reminiscent of *Watchmen*."
—*Strange Horizons*

"James Morrow's bizarrely funny new book *Shambling Towards Hiroshima* turns the usual Godzilla paradigm on its head."
—*io9*

## SELECTED TITLES BY JAMES MORROW

**Novels**

*The Wine of Violence* (1981)
*The Continent of Lies* (1984)
*This Is the Way the World Ends* (1985)
*Only Begotten Daughter* (1990)
*The Last Witchfinder* (2006)
*The Philosopher's Apprentice* (2008)
*Galápagos Regained* (2014)

**Novellas**

*City of Truth* (1990)
*Shambling Towards Hiroshima* (2009)
*The Madonna and the Starship* (2015)

**The Godhead Trilogy**

*Towing Jehovah* (1994)
*Blameless in Abaddon* (1996)
*The Eternal Footman* (1999)

**Short Story Collections**

*Bible Stories for Adults* (1996)
*The Cat's Pajamas* (2004)
*Reality by Other Means* (2015)

**As Editor**

*Nebula Awards 26, 27,* and *28* (1992, 1993, 1994)
*The SFWA European Hall of Fame* (2008, with Kathryn Morrow)

The Asylum of Dr. Caligari



Cover illustration and design by Elizabeth Story
Interior design by Josh Beatman

Tachyon Publications LLC
1459 18th Street #139
San Francisco, CA 94107
www.tachyonpublications.com
tachyon@tachyonpublications.com

Series Editor: Jacob Weisman
Editor: Jill Roberts

ISBN 13: 978-1-61696-265-4

Printed in the United States by Worzalla

First Edition: 2017
9 8 7 6 5 4 3 2 1

To the memory of
DOROTHY VANBINSBERGEN
artist, booklover, cherished cousin

## AUTHOR'S NOTE

While in embryo this novella was nourished by comments and interpolations from numerous friends and colleagues. My gratitude goes to Eva Maczuga Letwin for the German, to Carolyn Meredith for the Latin, to John Develin for his knowledge of painting, and to the rest of you—Joe Adamson, Justin Fielding, Daryl Gregory, Christopher Morrow, Glenn Morrow, Jill Roberts, Kevin Slick, Dave Stone, Jacob Weisman—for your invaluable suggestions and improvements. I want especially to thank my beloved wife and indefatigable in-house editor, Kathryn Morrow.

This is a work of fiction and, more to the point, of fantasy. The presentation of mental illness found herein is not intended to correspond to reality, being keyed instead to Expressionist art, Weimar cinema, and my own philosophical preoccupations.

# THE ASYLUM OF DR. CALIGARI

JAMES MORROW

TACHYON PUBLICATIONS
*San Francisco*

*Hegel remarks somewhere that all great world-historic facts and personages appear, so to speak, twice. He forgot to add: the first time as tragedy, the second time as farce.*

—Karl Marx

# ONE

From its birth during the Age of Reason until its disappearance following the Treaty of Versailles, the tiny principality of Weizenstaat lay along the swampy seam between the German Empire and the Grand Duchy of Luxembourg like an embolism lodged in an artery. Ruled by a succession of harmless hereditary monarchs whose congenital mediocrity enabled their respective parliaments to run the county without royal interference, Weizenstaat was for many generations a prosperous and idyllic land. Then came the Great War, and when it was over this polyglot nation had simply ceased to exist, annexed by Luxembourg without the consent of the principality's citizens, who were accorded the same measure of control over their fate that a cow enjoys in an abattoir.

Prior to its dissolution, Weizenstaat was known primarily for three institutions: bedrock political neutrality, a banking system sympathetic to the requirements of monopoly capitalism, and a sanitarium called Träumenchen Asylum. So successful were the treatments pioneered at this *maison de santé*—most famously the eponymous Caligari system—

the people of Weizenstaat took to joking that their country's principal import was irrationality and its principal export rehabilitated lunatics.

My personal journey to Träumenchen began many miles from Weizenstaat, at the 69th Regiment Armory in midtown Manhattan. On the 17th of February, 1913, the Armory opened its doors to a month-long exhibition of modern European paintings and sculptures (complemented by some indigenous pieces), the most audacious such show ever to disturb the digestion of an American critic. Having recently graduated from the Pennsylvania Academy of Fine Arts in Philadelphia, aflame with the naïve notion that avant-garde images were destined to cure the complacency of the bourgeoisie, I could no more have passed up this landmark event than the moon could waltz free of its orbit.

Because my story is inextricably linked to the Great War, its genesis in a military reservist training facility seems poetic to me. The Armory Show changed my life. It changed many lives. Words can never convey the exhilaration of my encounter with Marcel Duchamp's *Nude Descending a Staircase*, that fragmented Cubist figure in whom the sensual and the mechanistic existed in such riveting equipoise. My pen will never rise adequately to the occasion of Henri Rousseau's *Jaguar Attacking a Horse*, the violent event playing out in a jungle at once savage and serene. No earthly language is equal to Bourdelle's gilded bronze masterpiece, *Herakles the Archer*, the demigod taking aim at the

Stymphalian birds while balanced on a rock from which he has seemingly sculpted himself.

So what does a bookish farm boy from central Pennsylvania do upon realizing his eyes are in love with Pablo Picasso's *Woman with Mustard Pot*? He learns to speak rudimentary French, borrows two hundred dollars from his doting Aunt Lucy, assembles a portfolio of his best charcoal sketches, watercolors, and unframed oils (most of them tableaux of urban life rendered in his impression of Impressionism), and finds a job peeling potatoes aboard a freighter bound for Le Havre.

My crossing occurred without mishap. I proceeded directly to Paris by train, hoping to locate Señor Picasso and perhaps find employment as his apprentice. Although my Pennsylvania Academy diploma read "Francis J. Wyndham," I'd decided to represent myself as "Zoltan Ziska, descended from a line of North American gypsies famous for their spare but powerful folk art."

Things did not go as planned. Enraged by my presumption, Picasso escorted me to the second-floor landing outside his Montparnasse studio, threw my portfolio down the *escalier*, and, taking me by the shoulders, pushed me in the same direction. I tumbled to the bottom, humiliated but unharmed. Rube Descending a Staircase. As the *coup de grâce* he hurled a jar of azure-tinted turpentine toward my recumbent form (he was evidently still in his Blue Period). The glass struck the wall and, shattering, stained my white shirt with pale blotches. For several weeks I declined to wash the shirt, regarding it as a Picasso by other means, but in time I decided that the afternoon's true artistic event had been the spectacle of my ejection from the mad Spaniard's life.

Chastened though I was by this experience, I didn't stop trying to insinuate myself into the Paris circle. Despite my dogged persistence (which occasionally shaded into boorish impertinence), none of the other artists I tracked down assaulted me. This felt like progress. Marcel Duchamp spent a full minute perusing my portfolio, then furrowed his brow and said, "I suggest you learn a vocation, Monsieur Ziska, since you'll never live by selling your paintings. Brick-laying is an honest trade, and artistic in its own way."

Georges Braque was more considerate of my feelings. "I think that at present you paint like an American in Paris. Come and see me after you start painting like a Frenchman in Babylon."

Henri Rousseau was the kindest of all. "Whenever I am visited by a young artist whose work does not speak to me, I try to recall the lesson we all know from Hans Christian Andersen. Who am I to tell an ugly duckling he will never become a swan? Keep on painting, Monsieur. Something may come of it."

Of course such encouragement did nothing to alleviate my impecunious circumstances. Man does not live by bread alone, but it's a good idea to start with the bread. After three months of subsisting on restaurant scraps and street market discards washed down with public water, I was ready to enroll in bricklayer's school.

On a congenial July morning in 1914, I entered the atelier of André Derain, who had agreed to give me "ten minutes of my valuable time and a glass of second-rate Bordeaux." Derain was among the artists whom the critic Louis Vauxcelles had disparagingly branded *les Fauves*, the wild beasts (the most famous was Matisse), and while Derain's contribution to the Armory Show had struck me as paradoxically domesticated, a combination still life and landscape titled *La Fenêtre sur le parc*, I was mesmerized by the work-in-progress on his easel, an impiously Cubist interpretation of the Last Supper. Even more enthralling was his assessment of my work. In smoothly flowing English he called it "unassumingly intense" as well as "a portal to new possibilities in Impressionism." I nearly swooned, partially from hunger but mostly from the praise.

"Monsieur Ziska, I have a proposal for you," Derain continued, "a scheme that promises to free me from an awkward situation and improve your personal finances. I shall begin by requesting your real name."

"Zoltan Ziska."

"Bullshit. Isn't that what Americans say? *Merde de taureau.*"

"Francis Wyndham."

The Fauve took a drag on his cigarette. "Mr. Wyndham, did you read in *Le Soir* about the assassination of the

Archduke Franz Ferdinand, heir to the throne of Austria-Hungary? A Slavic radical, one Gavrilo Princip, shot him during a state visit to Sarajevo."

Although I had no interest in politics, I affected a somber countenance and said, "Oh, yes, an international crisis to be sure."

"Princip was a nasty little crackpot, and nobody much liked Ferdinand either, but the rulers of Austria-Hungary believe in punishing terrorist acts severely. Last Tuesday, with Germany's blessing, they declared war on Serbia and bombed Belgrade. Serbia's staunch ally, Russia, is mobilizing even as we speak, and Russia's staunch ally, France, is doing the same. Yesterday my conscription board told me I must put on a uniform, which means I cannot honor the commitment I made last month to Alessandro Caligari, the Italian alienist. Dr. Caligari runs the Continent's most celebrated mental institution, Träumenchen Asylum in Weizenstaat. He designed the building himself. I had contracted to become a teacher there, giving painting lessons to lunatics."

"Art therapy?"

"Exactly. The latest thing, very avant-garde."

"I'm flattered that you think me the right man for the job."

"To be honest, Mr. Wyndham, were I to leave Dr. Caligari's employ without providing a replacement, I fear he would exact some highly unpleasant retribution. Reading between the lines of his letters, I sense that he handles disappointment badly and nurtures grudges eternally. When in Herr Direktor's presence, pass up no opportunity to call Sigmund Freud a charlatan."

"Next you'll be telling me he throws people down stairs."

"He's not a Picasso, if that's what you mean. Patronize his eccentricities, laugh at his jokes, and all will be well. The position pays two hundred francs a week, and you'll receive free meals plus your own apartments in the asylum. I'll send you off with a letter of recommendation and the hundred-Deutschmark retainer I received from Caligari's private secretary. If you depart from the Gare d'Orsay early tomorrow morning, you'll stay ahead of the troop trains. Get off in Lyon and change there for Kleinbrück, the sort of municipality that in Weizenstaat passes for a city. Your indifferent French will serve you adequately, though the citizens normally speak German. Once you're inside the asylum, you'll be pleased to discover that English is the lingua franca."

"I'm impossibly grateful to you."

"There's something else you should know about Herr Direktor. He fancies himself an artist. He mailed me photographs of his paintings."

"And your verdict?"

"The man is not without talent. Despite his Italian heritage, his heart belongs to German Expressionism. His images are quite grotesque, shocking—horrific actually."

"Might we infer Caligari is applying art therapy to his own troubled psyche?"

"He may be troubled, but no more so than the gentility presently contriving to visit an apocalypse upon Europe. *Je vous souhaite bon chance, Monsieur.* God go with you—and with myself as well. I don't relish getting shot at by the Kaiser's soldiers, but it will be amusing to show the world that a Fauve can also be a patriot."

Forty-eight hours later, on Friday the 31st of July, I detrained in Kleinbrück, luggage in hand. As dusk dropped its chiaroscuro veil on the station platform, I hunched protectively over my portfolio case and made certain my wallet still held the vital hundred Deutschmarks. According to the last letter M. Derain had received from Caligari's secretary, the new painting master was to spend the night in the town, then arrive at the asylum in time for a three o'clock interview with Herr Direktor.

I faced the Moselle River, its spirited flow spanned by a wide wooden footbridge leading directly to a neoclassical marble building that my guidebook (a gift from Derain) identified as the Kleinbrück Kunstmuseum. A zigzag passageway, closed on all sides, with portholes instead of windows, connected the museum to a ponderous concrete edifice that was surely Träumenchen Asylum. Thrusting upward in a series of immense but ever-shrinking layers, the topmost surmounted by a bell tower supporting a gigantic clock (the whole arrangement oddly canted to the south), the sanitarium suggested nothing so much as a cake confected for some Brobdingnagian wedding feast. I'd been expecting a more graceful and therapeutically soothing structure, but who was I to criticize the great Caligari's vision of the ideal mental institution?

According to a map posted in the train station, the center of town was only three kilometers away, and so despite my burden of luggage I decided against hiring a private conveyance, and within the hour I stood before a charming hostelry called Das Blaue Einhorn—the Blue Unicorn. After securing my lodgings and receiving the key, I asked the clerk to arrange my transport to Träumenchen the following morning, whereupon his face acquired an expression of supreme dismay. When I asked what was wrong, he attempted to assume a nonchalant demeanor, then told me, in broken English, that if I was determined to work for Caligari, a hired car would be waiting for me at ten o'clock.

I ascended to my chamber, deposited my luggage beside the world-weary mattress, and, upon returning to street level, entered the diing room, where I ordered sauerbraten and a tankard of pilsner. Shortly after my meal arrived, a florid man sidled unbiden into my booth, assumed the opposite bench, and introduced himself as Herr Janowitz, the proprietor.

"Please sit down," I said in a sardonic tone.

"*Sie sind also geschäftlich* . . . I understand you have business at the asylum," said Janowitz.

"I'm the new painting master. Herr Direktor likes to supplement his methods—"

"As, yes, the famous Caligari system."

"With art therapy. I've heard his techniques are quite efficacious."

"Frequently an entire family will stay here prior to leaving a relation at Träumenchen, which means I've observed many a patient firsthand. I particularly remember a catatonic so severely afflicted it took three nurses to feed her. She returned from the asylum completely cured and eager to study modern dance."

"For a second I imagined you were about to warn me away from the place."

"Then there was the deluded young man who fancied himself Jack the Ripper. After his stay at Träumenchen, he became a tailor, sewing pieces of fabric together to make women's gowns."

"My employer sounds like a miracle worker," I said.

"A miracle worker but also, if the gossip is correct, a sorcerer," said Janowitz.

"This is the twentieth century."

"Not for people who choose to live in the Renaissance. It is rumored that Caligari dabbles in alchemy and occasionally raises the dead."

"At some point in his career, I imagine, anyone who heals by unorthodox techniques is subjected to slander."

"Did you know you had a predecessor? Werner Slevoght

from Bremen?"

"Let me guess. He went to work at the asylum and was never heard from again. Really, mein Herr, this is all too banal."

"No, he went to work at the asylum, and two months later Caligari arranged for his conscription into the German Imperial Army. The last time I saw Slevoght, just before he marched off with the Sixth Corps, he told me, 'The magician must be stopped.' I hope I haven't spoiled your appetite."

"Not at all, but if our conversation continues, my dinner will get cold."

"You have no belief in sorcery?"

"None whatsoever."

"Neither do I. What I fear are people who lack the good taste to disbelieve in sorcery and thereby end up practicing it. Enjoy your supper, Mr. Wyndham."

Although Herr Janowitz's warning about metaphysical anomalies at the asylum seemed ludicrous to me, like the rant of a decadent aesthete in a Huysmans novel, I awoke the next morning in a state of low-level paranoia. I ate a hasty breakfast in the hostelry dining room. The promised motorcar, a Daimler, was waiting for me, driven by a voluble French-speaking chauffeur who couldn't stop lamenting his son's decision to enlist in the Belgian Army.

Ten minutes later, having paid the driver and collected my luggage, I approached the Moselle River, its churning current spitting flecks of foam, then crossed the footbridge to the museum. The sign on the lawn read EINRITT NUR MIT EINLADUNG—Admission by Invitation Only—an assertion corroborated by the chain slung across the oaken doors in a stark iron smile. Träumenchen was likewise sealed, its windows crosshatched with metal bars, its ramparts rising at least twenty feet, its main portal fitted with a high steel gate. It made sense, of course, for Caligari to have conceived the place as much along the lines of a penitentiary as a *maison de santé*. Obviously the inmates must not be allowed to wander away and make mischief in the town.

A mustachioed guard inhabited the sentry box, his authority advertised by a holstered Mauser. He scanned my introductory letter from M. Derain with a gaze of quintessential suspicion, likewise the letter to Derain from Caligari's secretary stipulating the three o'clock interview, but eventually he allowed me to enter—the massive gate encompassed a door of begrudgingly human proportions—and proceed along a narrow, brick-walled lane to a second sentry box. Here I was again treated with gratuitous incivility, the beady-eyed armed guard perusing my credentials twice before raising the saw-toothed boom barrier.

Checkpoint number three was a cottage defaced by gingerbread decoration, beyond which a radiantly green lawn spread in prelude to a multilayered château. The grounds thronged with free-roaming inmates, some wearing costumes congruent with their delusions: Arabian sheikh,

Roman senator, Joan of Arc, Jesus Christ. The present sentry—a walrus of a man with a freckled face—was the rudest yet. After a protracted interval he cranked up his intramural telephone and proclaimed my arrival to whomever was on the other end.

Several minutes later two asylum employees appeared: a stately, stern-faced, white-coated woman with a stethoscope dangling from her neck like a pendant, her lips limned in red, and a tall, pale, cadaverous man in his late thirties, dressed all in black, his hair as dark and glossy as anthracite. To my eyes he suggested an autonomous shadow long since detached from its owner, or perhaps the Grim Reaper on his way to a ballet lesson. In impeccable English he introduced the female physician as Dr. Florence Verguin, the sanitarium's medical director, and himself as Conrad Röhrig, private secretary to Caligari.

I gestured toward the costumed lunatics. "Do I surmise that allowing inmates their delusions is part of their therapy?" I asked Dr. Verguin.

"Not really," she replied brusquely. "At Träumenchen we don't condescend to our patients. We cure them. Keep that in mind when preparing your art lessons."

As Dr. Verguin bustled away, Conrad Röhrig took my belongings in hand and guided me toward the château. Entering the grand lobby, I spotted more inmates in the throes of fantasy—a buccaneer, a Virgin Mary, a harlequin juggling rubber balls—and I speculated that such theatrianity would ere long acquire normalcy in my eyes. Conrad now led me along a crooked corridor hung with Gobelins landscape tapestries, until we reached a portal labeled KÜNSTLER IN RESIDENZ—Artist in Residence.

"Your apartments," he explained, unlocking the door.

We passed through the foyer into a sumptuous study filled with books and appointed with famous paintings (reproductions, I assumed), among them a still life tracing to Paul Cézanne's erotic relationship with fruit, a specimen from his celebrated *Bathers* sequence, and Edvard Munch's *The Scream*, the despondent, gourd-headed subject standing on a bridge at sunset, palms clamped against his ears and cheeks.

"The bathtub is capacious and the pipes reliably deliver hot water," said Conrad, handing me the key, "but I must ask you to consume it frugally." He gestured toward the Cézanne still life. "Do you know his boast, 'I shall astonish Paris with an apple'?"

Nodding, I secured the key in an escritoire. "He also said, 'The day is coming when a single carrot, freshly observed, will set off a revolution.' "

"The kitchen staff hopes you enjoy your lunch," said Conrad, indicating a tray on which rested a carafe of white wine, half a cold chicken, and a loaf of fresh bread. "A full breakfast will arrive each morning at seven o'clock, along with a recent edition or either *Le Figaro*, the *Berliner Morgenpost*, or the *New York Herald*. Naturally you will prefer the English-language paper. Dinners and midday meals are served in the refectory on the second floor."

"How can Caligari afford so opulent a facility? Are his patients all spoiled aristocrats? Is he in fact a sorcerer?"

"I had a notion Americans were brash and impolitic," said Conrad. "How silly of me."

We followed a narrow hallway to the sitting room, a sundrenched space featuring an overstuffed divan, a paint-spattered worktable, open shelves filled with art supplies, and an easel holding a blank canvas. Caligari evidently had an aversion to ninety-degree angles, for every pane of the high casement window was a trapezium.

"As you can see, your predecessor used this room as his private studio." Conrad indicated an icebox as large as a steamer trunk. "If you become hungry late at night, this amenity is stocked with delicacies. I shall return shortly before your three o'clock interview with Herr Direktor. Cézanne's remark about the carrot—was he being facetious?"

"I think not. He also said, 'When I judge art, I take my painting and put it next to a God-made object like a tree or flower. If it clashes, it is not art.' "

"One thing you'll appreciate about Dr. Caligari is that he never confuses himself with God—at least not on Sunday," said Conrad with a disconcerting laugh as he exited the sitting room. "As for his alleged status as a sorcerer, that rumor is certainly worth discussing, but not today. *Schönen Tag*."

Although the wine, a good Riesling, had made me tipsy, I managed a decorous ascent of the marble stairs to the fourth floor. Conrad graciously carried my portfolio. Our destination proved to be a high-ceilinged salon boasting an immense Persian carpet and a picture window overlooking an interior courtyard where inmates strolled in seeming serenity among elms and rose bushes.

Alessandro Caligari ruled the world, or at least the world of Träumenchen Asylum, from behind a mahogany desk covered with stacks of books, piles of psychiatric journals, and proto-Cubist carvings of the human figure by African tribal artisans. He was a stout and blockish man, reminiscent of Andrew Dasburg's plaster *Lucifer* from the Armory Show, with redundant chins, tumescent cheeks, a beetle brow, and round-lensed, black-rimmed spectacles behind which his tiny eyes lurked like skittish voles. His clothing was elegant, a black frock coat with a vest of green brocade. Despite his formidable features, he proceeded to install on his face a countenance so benevolent that a pastor would have gladly entrusted him with the role of Saint Nicholas in a church pageant.

Conrad set down my portfolio, placed M. Derain's letter in the alienist's grasp, and slipped silently out of the room.

"Show me your work," muttered Caligari upon learning of the Fauve's resignation. His voice was melodious though not distinctly Italian. "Lay your banquet before me."

I unlatched my portfolio and spread my Philadelphiathemed sketches and paintings across the carpet in a horizontal exhibition. Caligari rose and, aided by a Malacca cane capped with a boar's head, poled his bulk around the end of the desk like a gondolier navigating a canal.

"What do you call that one?" he asked, pointing his cane toward my watercolor of a beggar woman soliciting alms in Rittenhouse Square.

"*The Least of These.*"

"It's sentimental horse manure."

"Precisely my intention," I said, making no effort to conceal my annoyance.

"This is rather better." He indicated *Skin for Sale*, an unframed oil depicting a prostitute importuning a merchant sailor on the Front Street docks. "But the colors are too muted for so lurid a subject."

"I thought about using lurid colors, but I decided the result would be sentimental horse manure."

"This one works." With his cane he singled out my largest oil, *Step to the Rear*, which reimagined the mythic boatman Charon as the driver of a Market Street trolley car. "I admire any artist who would rescue Impressionism from prettiness. It's been twenty years since Monet started giving us his insipid water lilies, and he keeps revisiting the same damn pond. May I assume you've had classroom teaching experience?"

"None whatsoever."

"That hardly matters. Nothing could prepare you for

these students. You'll be taking over a class of four talented inmates handpicked by your predecessor, Herr Slevoght."

"Do you mean the position is mine?"

"If you still want it after the faint praise with which I damned your portfolio."

"I'm delighted, Signore."

"You'll meet with Slevoght's protégés every Monday, Wednesday, and Friday morning for three hours starting at nine o'clock. The classroom is on the third floor. North light, running water, a cornucopia of art supplies."

"I heard that Slevoght joined the mobilization."

"I don't blame him. The aesthetic intensity of this war will be beyond imagination. Even as we speak, European nations are manufacturing U-boats, battleships, military dirigibles, and combat aeroplanes like there's no tomorrow, the very condition those technologies are intended to secure."

"Did you say 'aesthetic intensity'?"

"A rare commodity." Returning to his desk, Caligari rummaged through the top drawer, then drew out a gleaming pistol. "I am fond of my nine-millimeter Glisenti, but it lacks the aesthetic intensity of a machine gun or a howitzer." He laid the pistol on the desk. "What do you know of our methods here at Träumenchen?"

"They famously eclipse those of Sigmund Freud, who I gather is a charlatan."

"I'm glad to learn his reputation is growing." Caligari unveiled a rank of large, gleaming teeth. "That Viennese cocksucker never should have turned his back on Charcot and the mesmeric tradition. The future of psychiatry belongs to hypnotism, not to some byzantine theory of sublimated fucking."

"And the future of hypnotism belongs to you, Signore?"

"Precisely," said Caligari, still beaming, "and to the brave new world of heteropathic medicine."

"I've heard of homeopathic medicine."

"Treating a disease by aping its symptoms instead of attacking the cause. Homeopathy has everything going for it except validity and results."

"Rather like Freud's system?"

"How pleased I am that Monsieur Derain couldn't accept the position."

"And heteropathy . . . ?"

"We charm the patient into embracing a self-image incompatible with the behavior that brought him here. Does he suffer from a split personality? Then convince him, through drugs and hypnotism, that he is the God of the Jews, that is, the most monolithic entity imaginable."

"Isn't that simply trading one form of derangement for another?"

"At first, of course, the patient may try to play the part of a Supreme Being," said Caligari in a tone of assent. "He'll devise a canon of commandments and entreat his fellows to obey them, but in time his spasms of dissociation and his delusions of divinity will neutralize one another."

"How ingenious."

"In cases of uncontrolled female sexual desire, we persuade the patient she is a Sister of the Carmelite Order," said Caligari. "Our nunphomaniacs, as it were, go on to lead surprisingly fulfilling lives." He removed a brass bell from atop his desk and, like a carnival barker soliciting the attention of fairgoers, shook it vigorously. "As for the average melancholic, he will show marked improvement upon coming to believe he's an actor renowned for portraying Hamlet, Prince of Denmark."

"Why not an actor renowned for portraying a clown?"

"You have much to learn about the human psyche."

Summoned by the bell, Conrad slithered into the room, a lock of black hair lying aslant his forehead like a scar.

"Before meeting your pupils in person, you should get to know them through their art," Caligari told me. "I shall conduct the tour myself. Herr Röhrig, please assemble Mr. Wyndham's portfolio and return it to his apartments."

"A powerful piece," said Conrad, offering an unsolicited opinion of *Steam Dragon*, my oil painting of a locomotive pulling into 30th Street Station. "It fuses the modern with the medieval."

"Herr Slevoght inspired his students to discover and colonize the nethermost reaches of their imaginations," said Caligari. "Any art therapist would feel lucky to have such accomplished lunatics in his class."

As the alienist conducted me down the jagged, portholed passageway connecting the asylum to the Kleinbrück Kunstmuseum, he searched through his pockets, soon finding a key so large it could have functioned as a palette knife. He unlocked the door. The space beyond was not so much a museum as a solitary gallery the size of a ballroom. Sunbeams poured through a trapezium-shaped skylight. Dormant gas-lamps protruded from the walls. The floor held a huge elevator platform suspended on four vertical chains threaded through pulleys attached to the ceiling, so that by cranking the adjacent winch a curator could deliver large paintings and heavy sculptures to the cellar for storage.

The room vibrated with art. Caligari was right about my predecessor's skills as an educator. Somehow Slevoght had inspired his students to venture into the wilds of their disordered psyches and then recollect their journeys through cathartic acts of creation. A row of six abstract sculptures cast voluptuous shadows on the east wall, a configuration bisected by the oaken doors leading to the outside world. "These pieces are by Ludwig Ruttluff, who travels about the solar system in his private rocket ship," Caligari explained as I approached the *papier-mâché* artifacts, each of which, though nonrepresentational, was manifestly erotic and arguably lewd. "Ludwig insists they are replicas of the indigenous sculptures he sketched while visiting the aborigines of Ganymede."

Sidling toward the passageway door, I surveyed the

still-life etchings surrounding the jamb: a chunk of rotting meat invaded by maggots, a shaving basin filled with cockroaches, a turnip bristling with rusty nails, and an apothecary's cabinet displaying phials of poison. "Like all paranoids, Pietro Barbieri is his own worst enemy," said Caligari. "Fortunately, his mind swerves so abruptly from one fantasized catastrophe to the next that his condition is not incapacitating."

The exhibition on the south wall included the work of a watercolorist who'd reimagined the three most powerful humanoid chess pieces—knight, bishop, queen—as berserkers armed with, respectively, a lance, a pike, and an ax, each weapon dripping gouts of blood. "Before losing his mind, Gaston Duchemin was a Grandmaster. Be prepared to hear all about Morphy's 1857 queen sacrifice to Paulsen."

Counterpointing Gaston's watercolors were three large spiderwebs, rendered in oils and mounted in decorative walnut frames, variously suggesting a mandala, a suspension bridge, and a maelstrom. In each case the spider herself lurked in the corner, waiting for a meal to become ensnared in her handiwork. "Ilona Wessels would have us believe she's the Spider Queen of Ogygia. Dr. Verguin and I aren't ready to disabuse her of that identity, for we can't decide whether her arachnophilia—or arachnomania or arachnofixation or whatever one might call it—bespeaks mere neurosis or an imminent psychotic break."

I couldn't assess the most compelling artifact in the

gallery, for it was occluded by a crimson velvet curtain draped over the top edge of the canvas. Was this painting so outrageous that Caligari had elected to censor it? At least thirty feet long and fifteen high, the mysterious panorama consumed most of the west wall, and I calculated it could be lowered into the cellar only if placed upright and diagonally on the elevator platform.

"Who created this magnum opus?" I asked Caligari.

"Perhaps Monsieur Derain informed you that I dabble in oils myself. I call it *Verzückte Weisheit—Ecstatic Wisdom—*from a chance remark I overheard the philosopher Friedrich Nietzsche make when he was a patient here. Yesterday I saw my painting under the skylight for the first time, and I realized it needs much more work."

"Perhaps you'd like to enroll in my class. Your first assignment would be to complete your epic."

"I appreciate the offer, Mr. Wyndham, but *Ecstatic Wisdom* must never be seen by our patients, not even your art students." He thrust his cane toward a staircase in the far corner. "Those steps lead to my underground atelier, and that is where I shall apply the final brushstrokes."

An emphatic rapping noise resounded through the gallery, as if someone were assailing the walls with a hammer. Caligari waddled across the room and unlatched the door to reveal a tableau at once entrancing and disquieting. Dressed in a yellow cotton blouse and loose gray Punjabi pants, a zaftig woman perhaps ten years my senior stood in the jamb, pressing a sculptor's mallet against her bosom as a novitiate might carry a crucifix. Her ebullient red hair and vibrant features—gazelle eyes, mischievous lips, lofty cheekbones—put me in mind of Munch's *Vampire*, the most arresting Expressionist entry in the Armory Show. Saying not a word, she rushed toward her mandala web and assaulted the surrounding plaster with her mallet. The resulting fissures extended the web beyond the confines of the walnut frame, turning the piece into a kind of collage.

"That's exactly what it needed," said Caligari. "Francis, meet Fräulein Wessels, the creator of these magnificent spiderwebs. Ilona, this is our new painting master, Mr. Wyndham of America."

I extended my hand, but Ilona Wessels declined to grasp it. Instead she faced Caligari and asked, in halting but lucid English, "What happened to Herr Slevoght?"

"He joined the Kaiser's army," Caligari replied. "There's a war coming, Fräulein. Regiments are on the march. You're not supposed to be here."

"Doh ray me fah so lah tee doh," sang Ilona in a high and beguiling voice. "I have just escaped from Nurse Ianotti and her ghastly choral society. I'm her only soprano. *Zu schade*. May I tell you my parting words to her? 'Fritz teed his ray so fah up Lahme's doh she's going to have a baby.' " She tugged on my sleeve and moved her lips in a manner at once guileless and knowing, the smile of a Madonna with a past. "I am the Spider Queen of Ogygia, and *you* are so young,

Mr. Wyndham. Are you also shallow?"

"Callow?" I suggested.

"Callow."

"I've never been asked that before."

"I was callow once," said Ilona. "Then I went out into the world, and I didn't much like it. If you ask Herr Doktor, he'll tell you I'm here at his sufferance. If you ask me, I'll tell you I'm here because I have four eyes and eight legs."

"Your spiderwebs are extraordinary."

"Stay away from the world," said Ilona. "That is my advice to you, young Francis."

"Fräulein, you must give me the mallet," said Caligari.

"Why?"

"Because your mandala is perfect now, and I'm afraid you'll try to improve it."

"Herr Doktor, I bring dire news." She alternated her gaze between the mallet and the alienist. "Last night someone broke in here"—she surrendered the mallet to Caligari—"and humiliated your picture."

"Humiliated it?"

"Or is the word 'mutilated'?"

Seized by acute panic, Caligari rushed toward the west wall, then lifted the curtain away to create a narrow aperture between velvet and canvas. He dipped his head into the gap. Exploiting the situation, which I suspected she'd deliberately contrived, Ilona reached into her blouse and retrieved from her camisole an apparent duplicate of Caligari's museum key.

"Herr Slevoght entrusted his secret copy to me," she whispered, passing me the key. "If Herr Doktor finds it on my person, he'll be furriest."

"Furious," I said, then pocketed the key, wondering whether to betray Ilona's transgression.

"There's nothing wrong with the painting." Caligari stepped away from his magnum opus, letting the curtain slide back into place.

"Perhaps I used the right word first," said Ilona. "Your picture has on it seven humiliating specks of dust."

"Have you really seen *Ecstatic Wisdom*?" Caligari asked her.

"Goats romping across a field of clover," said Ilona. "Very lovely."

"Fräulein, I need a serious answer. If I were to say, 'Ilona Wessels has never seen Dr. Caligari's painting,' would I be telling the truth?"

"Don't you always tell the truth?"

"Even in its unfinished state, the thing might make you sick."

"I'm already sick."

"You must never look at it."

"How could I?" asked Ilona. "I have no key. I should return to my tongue fun now."

"Your dungeon?" I suggested.

"My dungeon. If Nurse Ianotti comes looking for me, tell her I've moved to Brazil."

"It's not a dungeon—it's your private room," said Caligari, pivoting toward me. "The prohibition applies to you as well, Mr. Wyndham. My painting is for an invited audience only."

"Will my name ever appear on a guest list?" I asked.

"*Ecstatic Wisdom* will bring permanent financial security to our asylum, but only if I restrict its exhibition."

"I'm eager for Monday morning to arrive," Ilona told me. "We have much to offer each other, young Francis. You will teach me what you know of art, and I shall teach what I know of badness."

"Madness?" I said.

"That, too."

Whereas my first visit to the Kunstmuseum had been a vivid and memorable experience, my inaugural meal in the asylum refectory quickly became the epitome of *ennui*. Although the food was appetizing, a smorgasbord featuring slabs of ham and heaps of sauerkraut, my dinner companions—the various nurses, orderlies, hydrotherapists, and groundskeepers who kept Träumenchen functioning—would admit no topic to the conversation that hadn't passed the inanity test. Clogged drains, invasive mice, truculent straitjackets, obstinate wheelchairs, the low comedy of bedpans: these phenomena and little else were deemed fit for discussion. I bolted my meal and exited the refectory at a brisk pace.

That night I was plagued by insomnia of a particularly

aggressive strain. Not only did sleep elude me, but I kept picturing my body lying awake in my luxurious canopy bed, while batwinged incarnations of melancholia, catatonia, paranoia, and dementia praecox swirled all about me. Inevitably I thought of Goya's etching of an artist asleep at his desk, head cradled in his arms, his dreaming psyche conjuring up a maelstrom of predatory birds and beasts. The caption on the side of the desk read, *El sueño de la razón produce monstruos*. "The sleep of reason breeds monsters."

Finally my own reason grew dormant, but after a short interval I came abruptly awake. My nemesis was music: an aggressive march, aboil with trumpets and percussion. I glanced at my pocket watch. Four-thirty a.m. Sensing that these frenzied measures came from the nearby gallery, I threw on my dressing gown and retrieved the secret key (which I'd hidden beneath a loose floorboard in the sitting room). I exited my apartments and, pacing myself to the march, hurried along a warped corridor, then down the involuted passageway to the museum.

The instant I pulled back the door, I realized my instincts were correct, for the music grew loud enough to stir my blood. I entered slowly, wary that someone might have lowered the elevator platform. My fear was well founded: a rectangular void occupied the center of the room, a cavity from which rose billows of steam, multicolored and redolent of oil paint, even as brassy quarter-notes spewed forth like acoustic lava. I fixed on the west wall. *Ecstatic Wisdom* was gone—

returned to the subterranean atelier, I surmised. The only evidence of the painting was the crimson curtain (it lay in a pile beneath the wainscoting) and the row of three iron spikes on which the suspension cable had rested.

Against my better judgment, but true to a characteristic impulsiveness, I dashed to the staircase and descended twenty crooked steps to a skewed landing. Here I paused, having obtained an unobstructed overhead view of Caligari's atelier, or perhaps I should call it his alchemical laboratory, for he'd covered the dusty benches and filled the cobwebbed shelves with flasks, retorts, alembics, and test tubes.

Propped on a pair of gigantic steel easels, bathed in the light of suspended gas-lamps, *Ecstatic Wisdom* presented its reverse side to me, a tract of blank canvas nailed to mahogany stretcher bars. The painting was likewise invisible to the quartet of seated musicians—trumpeter, cornetist, fife player, drummer—each man adorned with black lipstick and handicapped by a leather blindfold. Operating their instruments by touch alone, they were evidently supplying the master of Träumenchen with the mood he needed to finish his epic.

Caligari stood before a worktable, swaying to the music as he added ingredients to four beakers filled with paint, each positioned above a lighted Bunsen burner and held fast by a ring-clamp. A black cat pranced insouciantly amid the roaring torches. The first beaker in line, containing vermilion paint, received a wriggling red salamander. To the cadmium yellow the alienist added a twitching golden beetle. To the viridian he sacrificed a small glaucous toad. The ultramarine received a blue slug. With each fillip, the steam rising from the elixir thickened, the vaporous columns mingling with the preternat ral rainbow I'd seen pouring from the elevator hatch.

"Tonight, Cesare, we unleash the power of Kriegslust!" Caligari shouted above the clamor of the musicians. Apparently he was addressing the cat. *"Viribus meis, et vocavi te!"*

The alienist scuttled to the far corner of the atelier, where a stuffed raven was perched on a human skull surrounded by four eggs. He transferred the clutch to a basket, one bright magenta egg at a time, then brought it to his worktable. He cracked open an egg, added yolk and white to the vermilion brew, and dropped the vacant shell into a graduated cylinder. He cracked a second egg, spilling its contents into the cadmium yellow paint. Next the viridian pigment acquired an egg, then the ultramarine.

Cesare offered me a contemptuous glance, and for an instant I feared he might betray me with a hiss, but then I sensed that (as with the other cats in my experience) his owner's welfare was at best an intermittent concern.

Caligari stirred the burbling beakers with a glass rod. *"Ut excessus sapientiae, de vitam!"*

Employing a panoply of brushes, he painted with a fury such as I'd never observed in a fellow artist. For the nuances he used bristles as delicate as the threads of

Fräulein Wessels's spiders. The boldest flourishes required a tawny sea-sponge impaled on a spatula, pigment dribbling from its pores.

The sleep of reason breeds monsters. For many years the caption on Goya's painting had puzzled me. Was he saying that imagination must be constrained by rational intellect? I doubted that any serious artist would make such an argument. Perhaps Goya meant the opposite, that rational intellect, while masquerading as humanity's salvation, was in fact a narcotic that prevents our grasping hidden truths—shades of William Blake's riposte to the hegemony of science, "Pray God us keep from single vision and Newton's sleep." Eventually I happened upon Goya's own elaboration. "Fantasy abandoned by reason produces impossible monsters," he'd written. "United with her, she is the mother of the arts and the origin of their marvels."

*"Hominus age incitatos, hominus age rabidos!"*

Watching Caligari suffuse his canvas with whatever species of wizardry or variety of delusion possessed him, I decided his methods represented neither imagination bereft of intellect, nor revelation allied with logic, but a third phenomenon. He had seduced both forces into a condition of mutual betrayal, reason convincing fantasy that violent monsters were desirable, fantasy coercing reason into forsaking its tedious allegiance to facts.

*"Effundam spiritum meum in vobis, virtutibus! Perfectus es!"*

Now he began spinning in circles—like a deranged dancer, or a whirling dervish, or a man inhabited by devils.

*"Exicita te! Le petit mort! Eveniet! Le petit mort! Eveniet!"*

Suddenly I realized that from his fluctuating perspective Caligari might notice me crouched on the staircase. Step by deliberate step, breath by halting breath, I ascended to the relative safety of the gallery.

"Tomorrow, Cesare, it returns to the wall, there to work its wonders!"

*Le petit mort*. The little death. Orgasm as an intimation of oblivion. The phrase was French, but the experience, I had no doubt, was universal.

# TWO

As I fled from Dr. Caligari's lurid artistic ritual in the bowels of the museum, the bleached light of dawn seeping into the twisted passageway and the winding corridor beyond, I vowed to behold the finished version of *Ecstatic Wisdom* at my earliest opportunity. The forbidden picture had aroused in me the aesthetic equivalent of satyriasis. My curiosity was fully engorged. I would have to act discreetly, of course, lest Herr Direktor catch me surveying his magnum opus, terminate my employment, and demand to know where I'd gotten a key.

Just as Conrad had promised, a full breakfast awaited me, along with a copy of the *New York Herald*. When not scanning the headlines, I consumed four plump sausages (they brought to mind the military dirigibles about which Caligari had rhapsodized the day before), two boiled eggs, a fresh roll with butter, and a carafe of coffee. Austria was still bombing Belgrade. Germany had declared war on Russia. France intended to honor its treaty with the Czar. The British government, allied to France via an Entente Cordiale, had announced that if the Kaiser's troops marched through Belgium, thereby violating that country's neutrality, Britain would declare war on Germany.

The bell in the clock tower tolled six times, each peal so mournful it seemed to augur the coming clash of nations. I removed my dressing gown, then crawled into bed. Despite the caffeine in my blood and the visions in my brain—Kaiser Wilhelm's dirigibles, Fräulein Wessels's spiders, my employer's burbling beakers—a delicious drowsiness possessed me. Lark songs and cricket trills wafted through the open casement in the sitting room. As the war came ever nearer to Weizenstaat, I wondered, would all such summer music be drowned out by bursting shells and exploding grenades? Perhaps, but for now it was mine to enjoy.

Three hours later I awoke, well-rested and in possession of a plan. I would eat my evening meal at the hostelry in Kleinbrück, then seek out Janowitz the proprietor (whom I'd treated rather rudely on Friday night) and inform him that the rumors about Caligari were true. The man indeed fancied himself a sorcerer, and Werner Slevoght's plea, "The magician must be stopped," was surely a *cri de coeur* worthy of our attention.

I donned my street clothes and proceeded to the grand lobby with its rotating population of delusionals (today's gathering included a buxom Cleopatra and an American Indian with three feathers in his headband). Stepping into the blazing August sun, I started across the immaculate lawn toward the gingerbread cottage. The corpulent sentry from yesterday morning was still at his post. When I told him I was going into town, he responded with a porcine snort and a practiced sneer.

"No staff member may leave the grounds without written permission from Herr Direktor," he said, stroking the handle of his pistol.

"You must be joking."

"I have no sense of humor," said the sentry.

"I insist that you let me pass."

"Your choices are to take up the matter with my employer or with my Luger."

A *basso profundo* voice called, "Herr Jerabek, that is quite enough!" An instant later Dr. Caligari, Malacca cane in hand, hobbled into view, his balding pate shielded from the sun by a crinkled stovepipe hat. "You can do your job properly"—he glowered at the sentry—"without resorting to bad manners."

"My apologies, Herr Direktor."

"Does this mean I may dine in town after all?" I asked Caligari.

"A reasonable inference, but incorrect. Please join me for a turn about the rose garden, and I shall explain why you must remain on the grounds."

"Signore, this is preposterous."

Caligari got his way of course—within the world of Träumenchen, I suspected, he always got his way—and for the balance of the afternoon we strolled through the interior courtyard enmeshed in an unhappy conversation. The lunatics took little notice of us, but on passing Herr Direktor the nurses and orderlies deferentially bobbed their heads.

"At some level our inmates understand they're outcasts from respectable society." Caligari indicated a patient dressed as a masked eighteenth-century highwayman. "It's salutary for them to see that we asylum personnel choose to live here twenty-four hours a day, so unworthy do we find that same respectable society."

"It sounds as if I'm a prisoner."

" 'Prisoner'? Such an unsavory term. No, Mr. Wyndham, you are part of the therapeutic Gestalt that makes this institution so effective."

"If I'd known my situation came with shackles, I would have sought employment elsewhere."

" 'Shackles'? Oh, dear, another unsavory term."

"I prefer it to 'therapeutic Gestalt.' "

"You are free to resign whenever you wish, although Fräulein Wessels will be disappointed. Our arachnophiliac is already half in love with you."

Before I could ask Caligari to justify his presumptuous remark, Dr. Verguin came marching toward us, clipboard in hand, stethoscope riding on her bosom.

"Good afternoon, Herr Doktor," she said, greeting Caligari and pointedly ignoring me. "We've had a breakthrough with Jacques LeBlanc on ward seven. He is no longer a bicycle."

#23  03-13-2018 03:21PM
Item(s) checked out to p31710189.

TITLE: The asylum of Dr. Caligari
BARCODE: 33029103402418
DUE DATE: 04-03-18

"I was just explaining to Mr. Wyndham our policy concerning extramural travel."

"Once the fighting starts, terrified soldiers from both the Entente and the Central Powers will be clamoring for the sanctuary only Träumenchen can provide," said Dr. Verguin. "You'll be grateful you're living safely inside these walls. Already we've had to turn away a dozen young men feigning lunacy."

"A German corporal tried to gain entry by posing as a catatonic," said Caligari. "Herr Röhrig dumped a bucket of ice water on his head, and that ended the charade."

"A French private insisted he was a bullfrog," said Verguin. "Nurse Ianotti exposed his ruse by presenting him with a live horsefly and inviting him to swallow it."

"If you're lucky, Mr. Wyndham, your native land will embrace isolationism," said Caligari, "and no conscription officer will come looking for you."

"So you don't think I would profit for experiencing—how did you phrase it?—the 'aesthetic intensity' of this war?"

"I can't imagine carnage becoming your preferred artistic medium."

"How could carnage become *anyone's* preferred artistic medium?"

"I think immediately of our former patient, the philosopher Friedrich Nietzsche," said Caligari. "Twenty-five years ago he went extravagantly insane in my home town of Turin. I personally arranged for his transport to Träumenchen.

There wasn't much we could do for him—he suffered from so many maladies: incurable sophistry, untreatable pomposity, inoperable honesty. I believe his essential problem was syphilis."

"What about mercury therapy?"

"We tried that, of course. He died fourteen years ago, age fifty-five. For Nietzsche this impending cataclysm, this transcendently meaningless war, would have been a gift from the gods. Nothing is true, everything is permitted, morals are nefarious, pity is for weaklings, so let us turn our lives—and our deaths—into works of art."

Although I dared not put my intuition into words, I felt reasonably certain Caligari was actually talking about himself.

The following morning, my brain buzzing with anxiety and anticipation, I entered my classroom at 8:00 a.m., a full hour before the students' scheduled arrival, the better to prepare for our first meeting. Under my arm I carried the *Bathers* reproduction from my study, for I planned to have the class copy it using oil pastels. The room featured four worktables, three potter's wheels, a lithography press, and a utility sink, plus a dozen easels arrayed along the back wall like a windbreak of metallic trees.

As I set the Cézanne on the chalk rack, it occurred to me that my intended lesson lacked panache. A quick tour of the supply cabinet yielded enough flour and salt for a considerable quantity of modeling dough. I combined the materials in two large metal basins, then added water and began kneading the mixture to form the required artistic medium. Upon completing the second loaf, I washed my hands, then placed on each worktable a rubber mat, a set of modeling tools, and a mound of salt dough.

The first pupil to arrive was Ilona Wessels, dressed in her customary yellow cotton blouse, a colorful madras bag hanging from her shoulder. Her current supervisor was the whey-faced Nurse Roussel, whose joyless presence had contributed copiously to the tedium of my recent meals in the refectory.

"*Guten Morgen*, young Francis."

"Good morning, Ilona."

"I've never sculpted before," she said, gesturing toward the nearest heap of dough. "Today I shall model your callow but intelligent face."

"I have a different lesson in mind."

"Ilona tells me I needn't fetch her at noon," said Nurse Roussel in an aggrieved tone. "She insists you'll be escorting her to lunch."

I looked Ilona in the eye. She reciprocated with a wink.

"That's right," I said.

Nurse Roussel shuddered, then guided me toward the door. "May I tell you my opinion, Mr. Wyndham?" she said, stepping into the corridor. "It's always a mistake to befriend a patient. Sentiment is fine, but science is better."

After her keeper was gone, Ilona sashayed toward me and laid a hand on my cheek. "This morning I learned something marvelous. Never have I hoarded so precious a secret."

"Pray tell."

"If I tell, it won't be a secret. If you pray, it would be a waste of time."

Now a gnomish orderly named Mittendorff, another of my stupefying mealtime companions, arrived with my male students in train. As they approached their worktables, I noted how perfectly these lunatics matched the mental images I'd formed of them while observing their work. Pietro Barbieri, the pudgy and paranoid creator of the disquieting etchings, was an ambulatory collection of nervous gestures, his fat fingers trembling, his eyes darting about like wasps in a bottle. Ludwig Ruttluff, our muscular and handsome space traveler, repeatedly cast his gaze toward the ceiling, as if longing to return to the stars. Gaston Duchemin, our hollow-cheeked, wild-haired Grandmaster, arrived spouting moments from Paulsen versus Morphy—"move six finds Black sacrificing a pawn at king four to avoid a fork and facilitate rapid development"—a behavior for which Caligari had mercifully prepared me.

"Who are you?" asked Gaston after the orderly had left the room.

"My name is Mr. Wyndham, and I'll be taking over this

class," I said, trying without success to speak in an authoritative tone.

"Where is Herr Slevoght?" asked Pietro the paranoid. "Did you murder him?"

"My predecessor went away to the war," I explained.

"Commander Ruttluff of Die Erste Galaxisbrigade, reporting for duty, sir," said Ludwig, saluting me.

"As you can see, today we'll be making sculptures," I told everyone.

"Even as we sit here, the German Imperial Air Corps is arming dirigibles with bombs," said Pietro. "Tonight we'll all be blown to atoms."

"Please listen as I explain today's assignment. Having seen your work in the museum, I know you all possess prolific imaginations. This morning you will wander through the uncharted sectors of your mind until you encounter a strange and mysterious bird or beast—and then you will render it in salt dough."

"On the largest Galilean satellite, the natives look like penises," said Ludwig. "I'm going to sculpt the one-eyed king of Ganymede."

"No penises today, Ludwig," I said. "Your pieces will be dry by tomorrow, and then I'll have the cooks bake them in the kitchen ovens. They'll be cool in time for Wednesday's class, when you'll color your creatures using tempera paint."

Before I knew it, Ludwig had left his worktable, dashed to the front of the room, and climbed atop a chair. "I shall be your model today." He removed the sash from his trousers, causing them to slide down his legs and puddle around his shoes. "Upon doing justice to my manhood"—he toyed with the waistband of his drawers—"you will finance my expedition to Neptune by throwing coins at my feet."

"Surely you know that officers in Die Erste Galaxisbrigade must be paragons of decorum," I told him. "They never pose naked."

"Move seventeen: Black snaps up the pawn at king's bishop six, thus daring White to capture his queen," said Gaston. "Paulsen, a notoriously slow player, thinks for an hour before taking the bait."

Much to my relief, Ludwig restored his trousers, then jumped off the chair and resumed his seat.

At this juncture the tenor of the class changed abruptly, and the students began working with gravitas and an exemplary dedication to craft, pausing only occasionally to throw gobbets of dough at each other. When Ilona sneezed, Pietro accused her of spreading deadly microbes, but the matter went no further. When Gaston started screaming—"Morphy sacrificed his queen and won! He sacrificed his queen and won!"—everybody ignored him, and eventually he grew calm again.

As the clock on the wall crept toward 11:30 a.m., I announced that we would now share our work.

Pietro went first, standing before the class and holding up a kind of swollen centipede, its numerous legs extending from each side of its segmented body like oars on a trireme. "Last night the mad Russian monk Rasputin released millions of pikeworms into our plumbing, each no bigger than a flea. Drink from the faucets, and your stomach will be devoured from the inside out."

Next Gaston addressed his fellow students, showing them a winged bipedal crocodile. "In ancient Akkad, realm of Sargon the Great, the knights occupied the squares now reserved for the bishops' pawns, and *these* creatures claimed the squares adjacent to the rooks. A dreadnacht could fly diagonally over three spaces, then abruptly change course and land two spaces to the left or right. The piece proved so terrifying that King Sargon made it illegal."

"The dominant life form on Callisto is the mellorope, a bird with multiple syrinxes," said Ludwig, presenting a flamingo-like creature whose long neck resembled three flutes welded end to end. "When she sings, you would insist you were hearing a pipe organ."

"This is the egg from which my grandmother, the first Spider Queen, was hatched," said Ilona, displaying an ovoid sculpture. The narrow end was breached by two spindly legs framing a head with four eyes and a daunting pair of fangs. "On reaching maturity, she wove a tapestry so beautiful it made stones weep. When the tapestry was eaten by moths, the kingdom mourned for a year."

"Ilona, why is your brain filled with spiders?" asked Ludwig.

"She has a disease called arachnophilia," said Pietro.

"It's not a disease," I said.

"Two days after I arrived here," Ilona told the class, "Dr. Caligari hypnotized me, hoping my subconscious mind would offer clues to my fixation, but evidently I'm just as crazy below as above. And now we must all applaud our new painting master, for he is a worthy successor to Herr Slevoght."

The Spider Queen clapped vigorously, thereby eliciting from the other students puzzled frowns and bewildered faces. My self-confidence survived the rebuff. Earlier this morning the alluring Ilona had professed a desire to sculpt my callow but intelligent face, and I asked nothing more of the day.

On the stroke of noon Herr Mittendorff returned to the classroom. To my utter astonishment, the students' sculptures drew from him smiles of delight and peals of naïve but sincere laughter. "Mr. Wyndham, I have no idea what these creatures are supposed to be," he exclaimed, "but I think they're all wonderful!"

Upon resuming his composure, the orderly announced that lunch would be delayed by an hour while the kitchen staff cleaned up following a grease fire. Before my male students departed, I instructed them to place their respective pikeworm, dreadnacht, and mellorope in a metal pan for eventual transport to the ovens.

"Are you ready to hear my secret?" Ilona glided toward me and pressed her lips to my ear. "When Nurse Ianotti brought my breakfast, she told me Herr Direktor has left the asylum for the day, something about a conference with field marshals." She picked up her grandmother's egg and cradled it in her arms. "In other words, young Francis, we can go see Caligari's painting right now and not worry that he will burst in on us."

"Aren't I supposed to escort you to lunch?"

"You heard Herr Mittendorff. There was a grease fire."

"I have a secret, too, Fräulein. Early yesterday morning I used the key you gave me. I sneaked into Caligari's atelier and observed him finishing his painting."

"And what is the subject?"

"I couldn't see the front of the canvas. The angle was wrong. He brews his paints like potions."

"*Natürlich*—he is said to be a mystic." She placed the egg in the metal pan. "How do you know he finished it?"

"He told his cat."

I removed the *Bathers* reproduction from the chalkboard, securing it under my arm. Ilona and I descended to the ground floor and followed the tortuous corridor to my apartments. We paused in my study, so I could restore the Cézanne to the wall, then proceeded to the sitting room with its trapezium-paned casement window. Bending low, I retrieved the secret key from beneath the loose board.

"Your canvas is blank," noted Ilona, gesturing toward the easel.

"It's actually Herr Slevoght's canvas. I haven't found the time to paint anything yet."

"And what will you paint when you *do* find the time?"

"Certainly not spiderwebs. I could never compete with you. Perhaps I'll venture into Cubism."

"A question keeps visiting my mind," said Ilona. "Can a person make a truly great painting that represents only itself?"

"I'm not sure I follow you."

"I believe the answer is yes." She drifted toward the shelves of art supplies, then removed a pig-bristle brush, a palette, a palette knife, and two paint tubes, one cadmium red, the other cobalt blue. "A picture of this sort would not look like a flower or a starry night or a spiderweb"—she set the materials on the worktable—"and yet it would not be a child's scribble, either, or an Islamic arabesque, or a decoration on a Grecian urn."

"Nor would it be blotches of azure turpentine on a white shirt. Remind me to tell you about my encounter with Picasso. So what *would* your picture be?"

"An apocalypse of pigment." She seized the cadmium red tube. "A cataclysm of light. An eruption of primal—what is the word?—primal Dasein, sheer *being*, unalloyed Existenz." Leaving the cap in place, she pretended to squirt a glob onto the palette, then did the same with the cobalt blue tube. "Such a painting would give you feelings you'd never felt before and thoughts that grow new capillaries in your brain." Taking hold of the knife, she pantomimed mixing the red and blue globs into a purple lump. "None of the doctors around here know what I'm talking about. Even Herr Slevoght wouldn't take my idea seriously."

"I take it seriously," I said, and I meant it. Though apparently broken, this woman's mind was a wonder to behold. Better a cracked vase than a flawless beaker.

"Thank you, young Francis."

"During my training at the Pennsylvania Academy, I never heard of anything like your theory. Are you having second thoughts about seeing *Ecstatic Wisdom*? We could stay here and make paintings instead."

" 'Theory,' such a marvelous word." Ilona approached the blank canvas, brush in one hand, palette in the other, then loaded the bristles with the imaginary purple. "Together you and I shall create the Wessels-Wyndham theory of nonpictorial art."

"In the Armory Show, Kandinsky had an oil, *The Garden of Love*, that at first appeared to be entirely abstract," I said. "But then the viewer realized it told the story of Adam, Eve, and the serpent."

"Ah, so the age of the nonpictorial has yet to arrive!" She leaned toward the easel and ran the dry brush across the canvas. "Our theory will usher it onto the stage of art history!"

"Now it's my turn to ask a question."

Ilona painted another phantom contour. "From this day

forward I am a theory person, an explorer in search of non-pictorial epiphanies." She simulated reloading her brush, then began tracing a third invisible line. "In case you're wondering, the name of this painting is *Violet Silence*."

"Did Caligari learn *anything* from hypnotizing you?"

She froze in midstroke. "Nothing about my spider fixation. He learned that I hated my father, something I already knew."

"You *hated* him?"

"Yes, but not for the sordid reason you're imagining." She returned brush and palette to the worktable. "If Caligari had found a sex trauma lurking in my subconscious, you may be sure he would have informed me, and with great glee."

"Why did you hate your father?"

"I won't tell you that, young Francis. Not today. We have an appointment with *Ecstatic Wisdom*. I'm so happy we are making a theory together."

So we left my apartments and set about defying the master of Träumenchen. Cautiously we followed the zigzag passageway toward the museum. Streaming through the portholes, the sun decorated our path with iridescent lily pads. I held my breath and unlocked the door.

Slipping into the gallery, Ilona at my side, I glanced at the elevator platform, making sure it was flush with the floor. The door closed behind us. Occluded by the crimson curtain,

*Ecstatic Wisdom* was back on the west wall, keeping company with my students' sculptures, etchings, watercolors, and oils.

"On the count of three," I said. Ilona and I each seized an edge of the curtain. "Remember, it's nothing but pigment on canvas. Ready? One . . . two . . . three!"

In perfect synchrony we unmasked Caligari's magnum opus, then let the curtain drop to the floor. We stepped back several paces and beheld what the alleged magician had wrought.

At once panoramic and intimate, wildly Expressionistic and excruciatingly detailed, the painting depicted a platoon of twenty beautiful young men, rifles in hand, tramping toward an offstage battlefield. Their olive uniforms evoked no particular army (certainly none known to me), but each soldier wore his regalia with shining pride. The new recruits' faces were canted toward the viewer, and I immediately made eye contact with the first man in line. Against all logic, he moved his arm in a beckoning gesture (or so I imagined), even as I heard his voice in my head.

*Come with us, my friend. Join our sacred brotherhood. Heed the call to arms. You need this battle. You desire it more than life itself.*

"When I saw Caligari cooking his pigments, he spoke of Kriegslust," I said.

"The love of war," said Ilona, nodding. "The craving for battle. I saw it in my younger brother and all my former husbands."

I broke with the soldier's gaze and fixed on the background. Beneath a blue and cloudless sky, fearless battalions marched, noble horses pulled artillery, and flags of uncertain provenance—all stars and swords and shocks of wheat—fluttered in an orgiastic wind. Now the gallery resounded with the same stirring fife, drum, and brass through which Caligari had brought the panorama to completion, and soon desires such as only soldiering could satisfy were churning through my veins.

"I need this battle," I wheezed.

"Young Francis, I must say that I, too, find the picture very—what is the word?—very excitable," said Ilona between parched gasps.

"Exciting."

"Exciting and stimulatory."

"Do you mean you wish to join these soldiers?"

"No, I wish to go to the dark gods!"

Now the platoon broke into song. Although the soldiers' uniforms were generic, the lyrics were unmistakably German.

*Solang ein Tropfen Blut noch glüht,*
*Noch eine Faust den Degen zieht,*
*Und noch ein Arm die Büchse spannt,*
*Betritt kein Feind hier deinen Strand!*

" 'As long as a drop of blood still glows,' " sang Ilona, alternately translating and hyperventilating, " 'a fist still draws the sword, and one arm still holds the rifle, no enemy will here enter your shore!' "

In a gesture of supreme sensuality she undid the topmost button—an elegant little mother-of-pearl disc—of her yellow blouse. An instant later the platoon began singing "La Marseillaise."

*Allons enfants de la Patrie,*
*Le jour de gloire est arrivé!*
*Contre nous de la tyrannie,*
*L'étendard sanglant est levé!*

" 'Arise, children of the Fatherland—the day of glory has arrived!' " I shouted as a lump formed in my throat.

Ilona undid a second mother-of-pearl button. "Please, young Francis, you do not need a battle today!" She grasped my hand and pressed it squarely against her left breast. I could feel her nipple through the fabric. "You will never need a battle! We must fuck ourselves free of Caligari!"

" 'Against us tyranny's bloody banner is raised!' " I sang, my bones and tissues quavering with Kriegslust.

She lunged at me, and together we tumbled to the floor. The next thing I knew I was kissing her on the lips and undoing the third button.

"Fuck flags!" she cried. "Fuck fatherlands! Fuck me!"

Despite the lovely buttons beneath my fingers, despite my wild oscillations between carnal arousal and martial rapture, I managed to entertain a rational thought. We must remove the evidence of our intrusion or risk Caligari's wrath. I rolled away from Ilona and, rising, grabbed one hem of the crimson curtain. She gained her feet and seized the other side. After three failed attempts we hurled the veil over the top of the stretcher frame. The velvet unfurled, momentarily quelling the painting's performance (no more music, no more singing) but doubtless leaving its powers undiminished.

Ilona took my hand and attempted to lead me away. For a brief instant I resisted, mired in Kriegslust, but then the better passion won, and we dashed out the door.

Standing in my study before Cézanne's magnificent apples, we sculpted one another with feverish fingers. Avidly I removed the layers of fabric—yellow blouse, silk camisole, Punjabi pants—covering the emerging pentimento of her flesh. With equal zeal she peeled away my blue flannel shirt and brown corduroy trousers. Apprehending Ilona in all her splendor, this Spider Queen with her lavish breasts, alert nipples, and impossibly desirable thighs, I felt confident that Caligari's painting would never possess me again.

"Someday I would like to own a satin gown," she said.

"Someday I would like to buy you one," I said, leading her into the bedroom.

"It will be the color of my hair."

"I'm having qualms," I confessed.

"Though I see the news has not yet reached your loins," said Ilona.

"Perhaps we should postpone all this?"

"I believe it was Martin Luther who said, 'It is better to sin boldly than not to sin at all.' "

Like athletes hurling their overheated flesh into a mountain lake, we toppled onto the mattress. Ilona reached between her thighs and lifted away the napkin through which she'd stanched her menstrual flow. She grasped my awestruck cock and drew it toward her, stirring her labia like an alchemist applying pestle to mortar. I decided this must be how the artists and poets of Paris disported themselves in their bohemian garrets. We fucked strenuously, nullifying Caligari's brushstrokes one by one, eventually achieving *le petit mort*, and then we did it again. Vive la France.

" '*Betritt kein Feind hier deinen Strand*,' " sang Ilona, then took my prick, stippled with her blood, and clothed it with her mouth. She bobbed her head up and down, her lips sealed around my *glans penis* (today even Latin was a sensual language), all the while moving her curled palm along the length of my ardor as if she were polishing a candlestick.

*"Formidable!"* I reported in French, spasming.

As the lubricious afternoon progressed, we became our own private museum, a gallery of forbidden sculpture, pose after pose, entrance by invitation only. Periodically we visited the icebox in the sitting room, gorging on cheese and dried figs, bathing our brains in Riesling, serving ourselves untoward portions of strudel. Seated beside Ilona on the divan, intoxicated by the raw fact of her presence, her Existenz, I alternated my gaze between her physical facticity and the invisible purple oil she'd wrought and titled *Violet Silence*.

"I believe I'm beginning to understand our theory," I said, pointing toward the canvas. Technically it was no longer blank; streaming through the casement window, the sun cast the shadow of a tree limb on the surface.

"Next time I shall dare to use paint," she said.

Not only did the icebox satiate our hunger, it abetted our bacchanal. Returning to the canopy bed with our spoils, we adorned each other with strawberry preserves and clotted cream. "I have memorized you," said Ilona, fixing me with the emphatic stare of Cesare the cat. "I have etched you on my retinas, every line and hair and pore." She climbed out of bed and, retrieving a hand mirror from her madras bag, held it before my face. "One day I shall be compelled to paint your portrait."

We proceeded to the bathroom. The tub was as large as Conrad had promised, and the water indeed proved delectably hot. Slowly, languidly, we washed away the residue of our pleasure.

"It is very awkward having eight legs, but I manage," said Ilona. "I can't recommend four eyes, either. I see too much."

"Ilona, you don't actually believe—"

"And now I must go to my tongue fun—"

"Your dungeon."

"Before Nurse Roussel comes pounding on your door, looking for her lost lunatic."

She hauled herself free of the tub, her limbs tinted rose by the hot water, her back and shoulders glossy with her ablutions. Upon collecting her clothes, she availed herself of a freshly laundered Turkish towel from the linen closet and a new menstrual pad from her madras bag. She dressed hurriedly. I followed her into the foyer.

"How marvelous that we have both of them in our lives," she said.

"Both of what?"

"Theory and fucking. Reason and Eros. I am so glad we are friends, and yet my heart is filled with sorrow."

"Don't be sad, Ilona."

"There is something so gloriously ordinary about friendship"—she opened the door—"and gloriously ordinary things are forbidden to the Spider Queen of Ogygia."

"I shall always be your friend."

"I don't believe that."

"How could I forsake the person who rescued me from Caligari's art?"

"Last week Commander Ludwig told me an interesting fact." She stepped into the corridor. "The asteroid Eros comes closer to Earth than any celestial body except the moon."

Given Herr Mittendorff's enthusiasm for Ludwig's mellorope, Gaston's dreadnacht, Pietro's pikeworm, and Ilona's arachnid grandmother, I did not hesitate to approach him after dinner and request his assistance in bringing the sculptures to the next stage in their evolution. He replied that he would indeed be happy to remove the metal pan of impossible creatures from my classroom tomorrow, deliver it to the kitchen, and have the cooks bake the pieces for two hours in a slow oven. I considered asking him to take particular care with Fräulein Wessels's spider egg, but I did not wish to betray the probability that I was falling in love with her.

Although Ilona's passion had surely put my Kriegslust in remission, and perhaps cured it completely, my dream that night betrayed a mind marooned in angst. With no aim beyond the rewards of perversity, my subconscious self opened the wax repository in my classroom and smashed the lunatics' unfired sculptures to bits. An instant later the dream took me to my study, where I scissored an apple out of the Cézanne still life and ate it. As the dream dissipated, I transferred all the unframed oils from my portfolio to the asylum courtyard, soaked them in kerosene, and made a burnt offering to the gods of modern art.

Shortly after dawn my apartments began reverberating with the steady tramp-tramp-tramp of numerous feet. I put on my shirt and trousers, then rushed out the door, sprinted along the corridor, and pursued the passageway to the gallery door. Caligari had posted a guard, the same obese and freckled sentry who'd threatened me with his Luger on Sunday afternoon.

"I need to analyze the work of my student Ludwig Puttluff," I said, speaking above the thunderous cadence.

"Not at six o'clock in the morning you don't," said the sentry.

"His sculptures hold clues that may lead to his cure."

"Today's exhibition is for soldiers only. *Geh weg, mein Herr.*"

Accepting this momentary defeat, I strode away, intending to reconnoiter the château grounds and perhaps solve the mystery of the marching troops. Reaching the grand lobby, which was crowded even at this early hour, I observed that the tramping had inspired a half-dozen inmates to strut back and forth holding phantom rifles and exchanging flamboyant salutes. An agitated Conrad Röhrig stood beside a potted aspidistra, the remnant of a cigarette balanced on his lower lip.

"Can you tell me what's going on?" I asked.

"No, but I can tell you that early on Sunday morning Herr Mittendorff saw you leaving the gallery." Conrad stepped away from the aspidistra and, aiming his dormant cigarette like a dart, hurled it into the flowerpot. "Perhaps you were inspecting Caligari's secret picture?"

"I was disoriented."

"It's a confusing passageway," he said in an amicably conspiratorial tone. "Perhaps you would like to join me as I attempt to fathom why Herr Direktor has brought hundreds of soldiers to Kleinbrück?"

"Indeed."

He led me to the north wing of the château, its walls lined with tapestries depicting troubadours in walled gardens. Upon reaching his apartments, he dashed inside, then returned gripping a pair of field glasses.

A half-hour later, having ascended thirty flights of stairs, we stepped breathless and perspiring from the topmost landing to the roof of the asylum. Gingerly we made our way along the parapet surrounding the clock tower. I glanced at the mammoth timepiece, which suggested some fabulous disc-shaped flying apparatus out of Ludwig's fantasies (its harpoon hands poised to spin madly and launch the machine into outer space), then joined Conrad in studying the peculiar maneuvers unfolding just beyond the château walls.

Two parallel columns of soldiers were on the march, the near one entering the museum, there presumably to behold *Ecstatic Wisdom*, the far line exiting and then returning to Kleinbrück Station. Conrad passed me the field glasses. I worked the focus knob, resolving the blur into a network of railroad tracks bisected by gravel paths (an image that for me evoked the Wessels-Wyndham theory of nonpictorial art). I panned the glasses past a water tower, a semaphore signal, and a row of tank cars apparently waiting to carry petrol to the emergent Western Front. The troop train stood idly on a siding, its locomotive swathed in steam, its twenty coaches dispatching and receiving young men in dull green German Imperial Army uniforms.

I surveyed a half-dozen soldiers as they tramped toward the river, crossed the footbridge, and disappeared through the open doors to the gallery. No man carried a rifle or pack; they were going to an art exhibition, after all, not a battlefield. Their patches and chevrons identified them as privates, corporals, and sergeants—from the IV Corps, Second Division, 3rd and 6th Regiments—but a few commissioned officers were also on the scene: captains, majors, and colonels, setting the pace by banging their riding crops and swagger sticks against rocks and tree trunks.

I handed Conrad the field glasses, and for a full minute he observed the troops as they emerged from their encounter with Caligari's magnum opus.

"What sort of picture does Herr Direktor have on display?" he asked.

"A panorama pulsing with Kriegslust. The pigments are evidently bewitched. He calls it *Ecstatic Wisdom*."

"It has changed these poor schoolboys." Conrad pressed the field glasses into my grasp. "And not for the better."

"I believe that's the whole point."

"So the great medical genius, healer of madmen, sorcerer extraordinaire, has elected to soil himself with history."

"History is paying him well," I said. "On Saturday he told me his painting will bring permanent financial security to Träumenchen—but he also speaks of aesthetic intensity: I'm afraid he sees this war as a grand-scale Nietzschean work of art."

"Yes, that would be Caligari."

I scrutinized the transmogrified soldiers. One instant they looked stupefied, automata in thrall to the painting, and the next they radiated a boundless desire to find a battle, any battle, and hurl themselves into its maw. How pitiable they were, these golden lads going off to die with no Spider Queens on hand to deliver them through Eros.

The clock hands locked onto the new hour, seven a.m. As the bell began to toll, I steeled myself, lest the vibrations waft me over the parapet. With each ponderous gong I could sense *La Belle Époque* slipping further away, torpedoed by U-boats, bombed by dirigibles. For all I knew, Cézanne really believed a freshly observed carrot would one day set off a revolution, but just then the world faced a more carnivorous sort of crisis.

"It's all about Soldatentum," said Conrad. "A difficult word to translate. 'Soldierliness' perhaps. Military service as a spiritual calling. Soldatentum is the state religion of Germany."

"And many other nations as well."

"True, but they're more subtle about it."

I shouldn't have been surprised when the mesmerized troops started singing, but their recital caught me off guard, and Conrad was even more astonished than I.

*"Solang ein Tropfen Blut noch glüht, noch eine Faust den Degen zieht . . . !"*

At this juncture I spotted Caligari himself, stovepipe hat squeezed onto his dome, feet planted on a grassy hill between the footbridge and the museum. Waving his boar's-head cane about like a *maestro*'s baton, clanging his ridiculous bell, he urged the troops toward their lesson in war appreciation.

*"Und noch ein Arm die Büchse spannt,"* chorused the Kaiser's infantrymen, *"betritt kein Feind hier deinen Strand!"*

After ninety minutes the parade finally ended as the last of the German soldiers, still singing, filed back into the passenger coaches. The doors slammed closed, the pistons hissed, the wheels squealed against the rails.

No sooner had the steam-driven behemoth rolled away, bound for some staging area or other, than another train arrived, its locomotive snorting and chuffing. Scores of unarmed soldiers spilled from the coaches, each young man wearing a deep blue French Army uniform—III Corps, First Division, 4th and 10th Regiments—and then the ritual occurred again: the parade to the museum, the enforced adoration of *Ecstatic Wisdom*, the return of the transformed schoolboys with their exultant faces and voices raised in song.

"Ah, so he isn't selling his services to the Kaiser exclusively," I said. "He means to infect all of Western Europe's armies with Kriegslust."

"And perhaps also the colonial armies of India and Africa," said Conrad.

"I imagine the Russians and Turks would be willing to meet his price."

"If I thought I could find another job, I would leave this place."

"How long have you been with Caligari?"

Splaying his fingers, Conrad racked his unruly locks. "It seems like forever. Before he discovered his mystic gifts, before he built Träumenchen, we used to travel around southern Germany and northern Italy together staging a grand spectacle at village fairs: Lorenzo the Hypnotist presents Giacomo the Somnambulist."

*"Allons enfants de la Patrie, le jour de gloire est arrivé!"* sang the French infantrymen.

"The show began with Lorenzo ringing his brass bell to summon a crowd, then directing their attention to an upright cabinet resembling a warped coffin," said Conrad. "Lorenzo would claim that for the past fifteen years he'd kept Giacomo in a state of suspended animation, lest the fiend go rampaging through the countryside committing murders. But in recent weeks, Lorenzo boasted, he had gained control of the sleepwalker's will."

*"Contre nous de la tyrannie, l'étendard sanglant est levé!"*

"Our employer has come far," I mused. "He got his start as a provincial mountebank, and today he commands a global war machine."

"After opening the cabinet, Caligari would awaken me and announce that the somnambulist was about to perform three amazing feats—swallowing a sword, eating a torch, and catching a bullet in his teeth. 'You can do this,' the hypnotist always told the sleepwalker. 'The spirits will protect you.' The feats were theatrical illusions, of course. But the fact that I would engage in these potentially suicidal acts proved I had no will of my own."

*"Aux armes, citoyens! Formez vos bataillons! Marchons, marchons!"*

"The climax of the show had me telling the fortune of anyone in the audience brave enough to ask," said Conrad. "I became skilled at offering the sort of cryptic prediction onto which a customer could project some deep personal meaning."

"Perhaps you would care to tell *my* fortune?" I said.

"I would prefer to tell Caligari's. 'Listen, Signore, I have gazed into the future, and I have seen that henceforth you will bring only ugliness into the world, and so you must take up your Glisenti pistol and do the aesthetically necessary thing.' "

# THREE

The big parade continued throughout the day and well past sunset, Caligari employing the gas-lamps on the gallery walls to illuminate his painting, or so Conrad and I inferred from the staccato glow pulsing through the skylight. About once every two hours a troop train would steam into the station and disgorge a column of soldiers. The magician remained on his hill, brandishing his cane and clanging his bell as the recruits marched by. Shortly before I retired for the evening, the flower of English manhood was made to experience *Ecstatic Wisdom*, hundreds of bemused Tommies walking open-eyed into the museum and returning ready to die for any flag the Devil cared to wave.

So rattled was I by the ghastly pageant that I canceled my Wednesday class and let it be known throughout the asylum that I'd contracted a respiratory infection. I spent the next two days hiding out in my apartments and experimenting with the Wessels-Wyndham theory of nonpictorial art. My first four efforts failed miserably, but the fifth—a torrid excrescence of red on a field of black—satisfied me, and so

I gave it a name, *Fearful Symmetry*, with a nod to William Blake's brightly burning tiger. I left it on the easel and stored its wretched predecessors in my bedroom closet.

On Friday I returned to the classroom and pursued my therapeutic obligations as best I could, but my mind was fixed on Caligari's marching somnambulists, to say nothing of that morning's *New York Herald* headlines: GERMANY VIOLATES BELGIAN NEUTRALITY followed by BRITISH EXPEDITIONARY FORCE HEADED FOR THE ARDENNES. I began by setting out the pan of baked sculptures—Mittendorff had done exactly as I'd asked—and supplying the students with jars of tempera paint. For the next three hours, the room hummed with the sort of enchanted energy generated by creative people working happily in tandem.

Herr Mittendorff arrived punctually at noon. Without a whiff of condescension he expressed a giddy admiration for Ludwig's golden songbird, Gaston's silver-striped chess piece, Pietro's polka-dotted parasite, and Ilona's jet-black ancestor. After the orderly had conducted his charges out of the room, Ilona rushed toward me, her lips arranged in a sensual pout.

"Young Francis, how wonderful that you have recovered from your illness, but I fear you are not yet incockulated."

"Inoculated."

"And that is why I told Nurse Roussel you will escort me to lunch again today. This plan raised both her eyebrows."

"As a matter of fact, it raises both my eyebrows, too.

There are ethical considerations here."

"I agree. It is ethically imperative for a mental patient to cure her therapist's Kriegslust."

"Also pragmatic considerations, by which I mean—"

"Yesterday I stole a box of prophylactics from the infirmary," she said, gesturing toward her madras bag.

So we descended to my apartments, entered the bedroom, and, despite the impropriety of it all, set about boosting my immunity. We entwined and talked with equal intensity. Ilona announced that she'd decided to reveal why she hated her father. I informed her I had momentous news concerning Herr Direktor's magnum opus.

"What news?"

Extending my frame fully along the luxurious goose-down mattress, I told her all about Tuesday's sobering events—the tramping soldiers, the troop trains, the transformation of tender young men into sleepwalking warriors.

"I heard the tramping, too, but I thought it was rats in the walls," said Ilona.

"I would guess that every German and Austrian field marshal knows about Caligari's war machine, and every Entente general as well, for what sane commander would deny himself the ultimate aesthetic weapon?"

"Young Francis, this wicked picture must be destroyed."

"I don't disagree."

"You 'don't disagree'? Can't you be less torpid?"

"Tepid?"

"No, torpid."

I contemplated her intricate face, its sculpted beauty defying the shadows wrought by the bed canopy. "Have patience with me, Ilona," I said at last. "I'm out of my depth here. Politics confounds me. Caligari says the war will be transcendently meaningless, and I don't know whether he's being canny or facetious or both."

"From what I have read in the *Berliner Morgenpost*, 'transcendently meaningless' sounds exactly right," she said with a brittle laugh. "We must devise a plan of attack."

"Assuming an attack is a good idea . . ."

"Of *course* it's a good idea. How much more transcendent meaninglessness can the world endure?"

"Getting at the thing would be virtually impossible," I said. "The parade occurs around the clock, and Caligari has posted a guard outside the gallery."

"Perhaps Herr Direktor, like Herr Jehovah, will rest on the Sabbath?"

"Perhaps."

We abandoned the bed and wandered into the sitting room, where we harvested wine and cheese from the icebox, then settled onto the divan. Still resting on the easel, my recent oil painting glowed in the silken afternoon light streaming through the casement.

"I see you've begun working with our theory," said Ilona evenly.

"I'm reasonably happy with it."

"Our theory, or your painting?"

"Both. I call it *Fearful Symmetry.*"

"Is it finished?"

"I don't know."

"This is not quite what I had in mind, young Francis, but you are stumbling in the right direction. I like the title. It invites the spectator to engage with the painting's Existenz by way of the tiger's Nichtexistenz."

I took a long swallow of Riesling. "Ilona, this is perhaps a crude and tasteless question—"

"I understand."

"You do?"

"The doctors around here are always asking me crude and tasteless questions. Why should my art therapist be any different?"

"Did Herr Slevoght become your lover, too?"

"No."

"I'm relieved."

"He likes only men."

"I see."

"Evidently he and Conrad were the best of friends, but that isn't why Caligari sent Herr Slevoght away. Dr. Verguin told me it was about philotopical differences."

"Philosophical."

"I suppose I loved Herr Slevoght, though not in the way I love you, and not in the way I hated my father."

She took a languorous sip of wine, then rose from the

divan and opened the icebox.

"My little brother Dieter and I came of age in a ramshackle chalet outside of Holstenwall," she continued, removing a cluster of grapes. "Father was a genius, a brilliant mathematician, but he was also a fool. He could have taken a university appointment—Georg Cantor desperately wanted him at Halle—but instead Johann Wessels spent his days sitting by the hearth, thinking about infinities, and in time I came to detest him."

"You mean infinity."

"No, infinities. There are many, as Cantor discovered. An infinite number. Mother gave piano lessons and took in laundry. Otherwise we would have starved. I have come to hate the idea of infinity almost as much as I hate my father.

"Infinity is a peculiar choice of enemy."

"But one befitting a lunatic, *ja*?" Ilona detached a grape from the network of stems. "Eventually Dieter ran away to Australia. Mother died of consumption. I survived two disastrous marriages and a third that would have failed if the bastard hadn't accidentally drowned. At least I inherited his bank account." She swallowed the grape. "As for Father—let's just say he never lost track of his service revolver." She approached the easel and pointed to the center of *Fearful Symmetry*. "Young Francis, you must place a dot of cobalt blue here. That is what your painting wants."

The following day, the Hebrew Sabbath, I ascended to the clock tower and once again observed the depressing spectacle of governments priming schoolboys for slaughter. By now the gray-suited troops of Czar Nicholas II had joined the mobilization, absorbing the painting prior to their deployment on whatever Eastern Front was destined to open between the Gulf of Riga and the Black Sea.

Then came the Christian Sabbath, and no mass mesmerizations occurred, just as Ilona had predicted, the generals and heads of state having evidently agreed to countenance the Savior over Soldatentum on the holiest day of the week. Ilona, I decided, was right: an attack was needed—and the dragonslayer, I resolved, must be myself.

I left the clock tower, the bell tolling behind me, twelve deafening peals, and hurried to my classroom. The bottom shelf of the supply cabinet held canisters of turpentine for cleaning oil paint from brushes, palettes, and fingers. I removed a one-gallon container and unscrewed the cap. An unmistakable fragrance razored forth, befouling the air.

As I resealed the canister and slipped it into my rucksack, I wondered whether saturating the painting with turpentine would really disable it. Could it be that, against those alchemical pigments, an ordinary solvent would prove useless? Might I need to immolate the monster? I rifled through the cabinet in search of matchsticks (essential for lighting the annealing torch employed in *repoussé* metalwork), eventually finding a box labeled *Streichhölzer:*

*Hergestellt in Dresden.*

Once back in my apartments, I drank two glasses of wine. Seeking to further distract myself, I alternately read Victor Hugo's *The Man Who Laughs*—my study came with an English translation—and worked on my nonpictorial painting. Ilona was right about the dot of cobalt.

Night came to Weizenstaat. With the stealth of a Schwarzwald wolf I slunk down the passageway to the gallery, the turpentine canister riding in my rucksack. The door was locked but unguarded. I opened it with Slevoght's stolen key. Silently waiting to ensnare Monday's battalions, the painting still hung on the west wall, its crimson curtain illuminated by the moonbeams glancing through the skylight.

While patronizing the museum, some soldier or other had knocked over a sculpture by Ludwig resembling a stupendous saguaro cactus. I set the piece upright, then secured the turpentine in the crook between the two largest arms. I removed the lid. Again the scent rushed out, abrading my sinuses.

Leaving the turpentine in place, I crossed the gallery, took a deep breath, and grasped the curtain with both hands. Like a matador flourishing his cape, I swirled the velvet in an extravagant arc, then let it fall. I averted my eyes. The singing began immediately.

*"Solang ein Tropfen Blut noch glüht, noch eine Faust den Degen zieht . . ."*

Fixing my gaze on the floor, I returned to the cactus

sculpture and retrieved my weapon.

*"Und noch ein Arm die Büchse spannt . . ."*

I charged the malign painting, waving the open canister back and forth like a deranged gardener wielding a watering can. Stinking streams of turpentine flew toward *Ecstatic Wisdom*, but instead of splashing against the canvas they halted in midair, a full yard shy of the stretcher frame.

*"Betritt kein Feind hier deinen Strand!"*

Against all logic, the suspended turpentine coalesced into a translucent sheet as large as a bedspread, even as the matchbox flew out of my pocket and hovered before me like the dagger in *Macbeth*. A single stick emerged from the compartment, then ignited itself. I dropped the empty canister. The matchbox fell to the floor.

Gliding purposefully, the lit match pricked the floating cataract, whereupon the turpentine burst into flames. As the fiery liquid veil flew toward me, it let out an unearthly shriek. Black acrid smoke filled the room. Coughing, I spun on my heel and sprinted away. The burning veil pursued me around the gallery like a pyromaniacal banshee.

*"Allons enfants de la Patrie, le jour de gloire est arrivé!"*

Whatever mystic principles drove the red demon, it was not exempt from the laws of physics. Before it could murder me, the veil ran short of fuel. The flames expired, leaving me shaken and nauseated, but alive.

*"Contre nous de la tyrannie, l'étendard sanglant est levé!"*

As if hoping to rattle me with a final demonstration of its

powers, the painting now caused the fallen curtain to rise and drape itself over the stretcher frame. I retrieved both canister and matchbox, then stumbled out of the gallery, a thumping in my chest, an embarrassment in my trousers, a knot of despair in my stomach.

From now until the armistice—though God alone knew when that would occur—*Ecstatic Wisdom* would rule the Western Front, the Eastern Front, and whatever additional murderous circuses the generals cared to convene. A half-dozen governments, and perhaps many more, would fill the sorcerer's coffers with gold and his soul with unholy satisfactions. Perhaps later in the century some other magician would devise a better-oiled and more efficient war machine, but for the time being Alessandro Caligari had the field to himself.

For Monday's lesson I removed the reproduction of *The Scream* from the wall of my study and bore it to my classroom. I set the painting on the chalkboard and, after equipping the pupils with hand mirrors, instructed them to copy it using colored pencils. But this was not a simple exercise in mimicry, for I required everyone to replace the shrieking figure on the bridge with a self-portrait.

"By representing yourself as the personification of despair," I said in a steady, confident voice (for I now regarded myself as a genuine art therapist), "you will be taking a courageous step toward rehabilitation."

At the end of the class, Gaston, Ludwig, and Pietro approached me and reported that, thanks to Munch's encounter with the abyss, they could imagine their misery one day progressing to mere unhappiness. But Ilona had resisted the assignment. Instead of superimposing her own features on the screamer's face, she had copied Munch's vision line for line.

"A Spider Queen is forbidden to portray herself in any medium," she explained after the others had left.

"My dear Fräulein Wessels, you aren't really—"

"What would you know of 'really,' young Francis? I've seen more 'really' in my life than women twice my age. If I want to stay away from 'really' until my money runs out and I have to leave here, then that is what I shall do."

Not until we'd secluded ourselves in the privacy of my apartments, contemplating the paintings I'd made prior to *Fearful Symmetry* (and analyzing their failure to actualize Existenz), did I tell Ilona about Sunday's fiery disaster.

"I should have been there to protect you," she said.

"I'm glad you weren't. You might have been badly burned."

"So what happens next, my darling?"

"Nothing happens next."

"You're giving up after just one attack?"

"It was one attack too many." Eager to change the subject, I showed Ilona the most recent *New York Herald* to reach my door. FRENCH ARMIES SWEEP TOWARD ALSACE-LORRAINE, ran the headline. GENERAL JOFFRE SEEKS TO RECLAIM REGION FROM GERMAN EMPIRE. "Tomorrow morning we'll read of the first engagement, and then another will follow, and another, and another."

My prediction proved woefully correct. Western Europe had begun to bleed. For the remainder of the month my life became a pandemonic carnival of teaching art lessons to mental patients (my assignments were uninspired but the students seemed to find them therapeutic), escorting Ilona to lunch by way of my apartments (thereby further scandalizing Nurse Roussel), and reading about the great Continental hemorrhage. First came a horrendous fight for Alsace, then equally gruesome struggles for Lorraine, the Ardennes, Charleroi, Mons, Le Cateau, and Guise, a conglomeration of engagements that the journalists termed the Battle of the Frontiers. Belgian casualties: 4,500. British: 29,597. German: 305,594. French: 329,000. In consequence of miscalculations by the French field marshal, Joseph Joffre, the Kaiser's troops were now overrunning much of Flanders, Artois, and Champagne. Owing to blunders by the German field marshal, Helmuth von Moltke, General Joffre had succeeded in transferring a large force to the west to secure the defense of Paris. Although neither side had won the Battle of the Frontiers, neither side had lost it either, except for those thousands of young men who'd been folded into the campaign's alleged necessities and inexorable arithmetic.

On the day after General Joffre achieved at Guise his late August *victoire sans lendemain*, his hollow triumph, Conrad appeared at my door and announced that Caligari wanted to see me at four o'clock that afternoon. With a heavy heart I told Conrad about my calamitous attempt to destroy *Ecstatic Wisdom*.

"I admire your bravery," he said.

"I don't. It nearly got me killed. What's the agenda for my meeting with Herr Direktor?"

"He didn't say, but I suspect it concerns your turpentine attack."

"God help me."

With surpassing trepidation I made my way to the fourth floor, convinced that Caligari had learned of my foray and intended to exact punishment. But as it happened, he wished to address a far more congenial matter.

"How would you assess the condition of Fräulein Wessels?" he asked, scrutinizing me from behind his desk. Cesare the cat pranced back and forth amid the African carvings and stacks of books.

"She's still the Spider Queen of Ogygia, if that's what you mean."

"Do you know what Freud would say about Fräulein Wessels? During infancy she channeled her libidinous impulses—"

"Freud posits a childhood sex drive?"

"It's a gaudy theory. Like all little girls, she channeled

these impulses toward her father, even as she cultivated an unconscious desire to commit matricide and take her mother's place in the marital bed."

"You're making this up."

"No, Freud is. His apostle Carl Jung applied the term 'Electra complex' to the syndrome. In the view of those two quacks, Ilona entered womanhood without resolving her incestuous fantasies, and so she became a delusional neurotic."

"We both know she had difficulties with her father, but not of the sort you're describing."

"Here at Träumenchen, by contrast, we don't *talk* about erotic fantasies—we enact them. And that is why you must instruct Fräulein Wessels to take up residence in your apartments."

"I must do what?"

"There's room enough for both of you."

"Signore, I don't understand."

"I want you two to start fucking until your eyes fall out—is that clear enough?" said Caligari. "Nurse Roussel will supply you with prophylactics. I call it *la cura amore*. I'm convinced that in Fräulein Wessels's case it's the best way to prevent her arachnophilia from advancing to hebephrenia, a personality schism, or some equally unfortunate disorder. Would daily encounters be feasible?"

"Signore, she is my student," I protested.

"Don't pretend you've come down with a sudden case of

scruples. Nurse Roussel reports that you and Fräulein Wessels are spending many extracurricular hours together. Tomorrow I shall instruct Herr Röhrig to issue your *inamorata* her own key. With every act of copulation you'll be giving the lie to Freud's talking cure—unless, of course, you agree with him that people can simply chatter their way to wellness?"

"I'm sure *la cura amore* is superior."

The alienist smiled and scratched Cesare behind the ears. "Tell me, Mr. Wyndham, do you stay abreast of current events? Do you read your newspapers?"

"Every morning."

"Then you know that the bloody fighting in Belgium is momentarily on hiatus. Soon we'll have bloodier fighting in France along the Marne River. Dr. Verguin has heard rumors of a pathology that first manifested itself during the Frontiers engagements, 'shell-shock' in the parlance of the army physicians. Don't be dismayed if you start seeing mentally wounded soldiers wandering our halls."

" 'Shell-shock,' " I echoed. "I imagine it's more real than the Electra complex."

Caligari favored me with a smile of approbation. "As even Freud could tell you, the human psyche is ill-equipped for crawling around in the mud day after day beneath artillery bombardments."

"Do you believe shell-shock can be treated with art therapy?"

"I would prefer to treat it with fucking, but we lack

the resources, Träumenchen being an asylum and not a brothel." Caligari ran the edge of his hand along Cesare's back, inspiring the cat to stretch himself languidly. "This meeting has ended. Go to Fräulein Wessels and enlist her in our conspiracy against the Freudian menace. Herr Röhrig will send me reports on your progress."

Although my explanation of why Herr Direktor wanted us to cohabit made little sense to Ilona, and I didn't really understand it either, she greeted the prospect with a smile as wide as Gwynplaine's in *The Man Who Laughs*.

"Naturally a person should hesitate to obey the wishes of the dubious Caligari, but *la cura amore* is so very beautiful I cannot resist," she said. "And yet, young Francis, I must tell you my great and paradoxical fear. The closer we become as lovers, the nearer draws the day when you will abandon me."

"I cannot imagine abandoning you."

"My first husband left me for a cabaret singer, the second for a gin bottle. Then came Gerhard, who fell into the Rhine and drowned while returning from the house of his mistress. I think you will leave me for a woman too sane to believe that art can grow new capillaries in the brain."

"I am yours for eternity."

"Please, young Francis, no eternities. They are too much like infinities."

And so she become my paramour in residence. When not

pursuing the measures Caligari had prescribed for constraining her madness, we spent long hours covering canvases with abstract forms and daubs that aspired to unalloyed Existenz. Some of our efforts were collaborations, Ilona grasping the brush in her dominant hand (the left) while I clutched the same implement in my right, the two of us contacting the canvas in tandem and allowing the paint-laden bristles to travel hither and yon like the planchette on a Ouija board.

But whether painting, making love, or attending to quotidian details, we could not escape the shadow of the adjacent Kriegslust factory. Before long the *New York Herald* corroborated Caligari's forecast that the next chapter in the Great War would be a series of engagements throughout the Marne floodplain. The journalists offered their usual clinical accounts of skirmishes and battles, attacks and counterattacks, complete with maps showing disputed ground and graphs referencing unfathomable grief.

" 'Casualties'—what a ridiculous word," I said to Ilona. "There is nothing casual about a young man being torn to pieces by flying metal."

As Caligari had also predicted, the Marne brought an influx of patients diagnosed with shell-shock. Träumenchen became a haunted place, its corridors clogged with inmates who seemed not so much soldiers as ambulatory corpses. In light of this epidemic, I was hardly surprised when, on the day the *New York Herald* informed its readers that a "stalemate" now obtained on the Western Front, Dr.

Verguin told me about Viktor Zimmer, German VI Corps, a battle-weary Leutnant—meaning lieutenant—she'd just finished evaluating.

"A difficult case," she said, absently fingering the resonator on her stethoscope. "The poor fellow insists on wearing a bandana around his mouth and nose, so chlorine gas won't get into his lungs—except the Entente doesn't use gas, not yet. Before the war he worked as a painter and printmaker, and I believe he would benefit from your class."

"The shock of artillery versus the shock of the avant-garde," I mused. "Perhaps the second trauma can ameliorate the first? Aesthetic heteropathy?"

"Assuming you and Fräulein Wessels can spare a moment from your sex regimen," said Dr. Verguin, "I'll have Nurse Roussel deliver Zimmer to your apartments tomorrow morning for an interview."

Twelve hours later, while Ilona soaked in her regular morning bath and I savored poached eggs in my dining room, someone knocked impatiently on the door. I took a swallow of cold coffee, then admitted Nurse Roussel and her unfortunate charge. Dr. Verguin had prepared me for Viktor Zimmer's gas-resistant bandana (it was bright red). The Leutnant also wore a muted green German Imperial Army uniform shorn of all insignia. His gaze was vacant. His lower legs jerked uncontrollably. When I guided him into my study and bid him take a chair, he replied, in a tremulous voice, "I've forgotten how to sit."

"At eleven o'clock, Herr Zimmer, you will report to the natatorium for hydrotherapy," Nurse Roussel instructed him. "Can you manage that?"

"I'll make sure he gets there," I told her.

"During the Marne I saw a hideously wounded man wandering around the battlefield," said Zimmer. "He'd lost his entire lower jaw to shrapnel."

"I know you've been through hell," I said, "and I'll do everything I can to help you."

The instant Nurse Roussel left my apartments, the Leutnant's demeanor changed dramatically. He removed the bandana and crammed it in his trousers pocket. A light came to his eyes. Calmly he extended his arm, fingers steady and solicitous. We shook hands.

"Yes, I've been through hell, but it did not destroy me," said the Leutnant. "My shell-shock, to use that dubious term, is largely feigned."

"I don't blame you for running away."

"I did not run *away*—I ran *here*, to Träumenchen. I'm more familiar with this place than you suppose. In fact, I once occupied these very apartments, and my real name is—"

"Herr Slevoght!" Ilona stood in the doorway to the study, her plenteous red tresses dripping water, her body wrapped in a white Turkish towel.

"Good morning, Fräulein," said our visitor.

"Is that really you, Herr Slevoght?"

"You're looking well, Ilona."

"I am becoming less sick," she said. "Mr. Wyndham is treating me with *la cura amore*."

"So I see."

"How wonderful that you've returned," Ilona told my predecessor. "You look terrible."

"Carnage does not agree with me. There is much we need to discuss."

"We have coffee and pastries."

So the three of us retired to the dining room, where we sat at the oaken parallelogram table pursuing a conversation fueled by sugar, caffeine, and immoderate anxiety.

"I'm told I acquitted myself well as a soldier," said Slevoght, sipping coffee, "but art will always be my primary passion—and yours, too, am I right, Mr. Wyndham?"

"Indeed. Call me Francis."

"Werner," he said, shaking my hand. "How I've missed the smell of linseed oil. I'm actually looking forward to attending your classes, assuming Ludwig, Pietro, and Gaston will pledge to keep mum about their former teacher's return from the front. Many are the faces of Werner Slevoght. Not only have I led two lives as an art therapist and a mental patient, I continue to lead two lives as . . . can you guess what I'm getting at?"

"Ilona told me."

" 'The love that dare not speak its name,' as a friend of Oscar Wilde put it. In the opinion of Dr. Freud, people with my predilections are as sick as any Träumenchen inmate. Caligari's dislike of the Viennese alienist is the only thing I admire about him. If Freud is a charlatan, Caligari is a megalomaniac—a more dangerous syndrome. Do you know about the ensorcelled painting?"

"Last month I witnessed Caligari's war machine in action," I said, "long columns of soldiers visiting the Kunstmuseum and leaving it afflicted with what Conrad calls Soldatentum."

"Yes, that's the right word. And how is our dear Conrad?"

"Sound in body but not in spirit."

"Poor man," said Werner. "He wastes eight years of his life touring Europe as a second-fiddle sleepwalker to Caligari's charismatic hypnotist, and *then* he becomes his drudge at Träumenchen, and *then* he learns his employer is a war profiteer."

"You should know that three weeks ago I tried to burn the painting," I said, biting into a *pain au chocolat*. "The damned thing turned my turpentine into a flaming demon. I was nearly incinerated."

"How did you manage to attack the beast with all those soldiers coming and going?"

"Caligari remembers the Sabbath and keeps it holy," I said, "though I wouldn't count on his maintaining that observance indefinitely."

"Has he given his obscenity a name?"

"*Verzückte Weisheit*," said Ilona, buttering a poppy seed roll. "Its effect on male spectators is always the same boring Kriegslust. On women—or at least on this woman—it exerts a more benevolent influence, libidinous rather than jingoist."

"I must admit, I find Herr Direktor's attitude toward the war difficult to fathom," I said. "He calls it 'transcendently meaningless,' which for him is evidently a term of approbation."

Werner ate a piece of his Streuselkuchen. "I never cared for Caligari's adolescent strutting. He got it from Nietzsche, I believe, when the philosopher was living here. Although my relationship with Caligari was strictly collegial, occasionally I glimpsed his project—*Ecstatic Wisdom*, you said?—when it was just a jumble of charcoal sketches and watercolor studies. Eventually I realized he intended to create a preternatural call to arms. And then one day he caught me leafing through the watercolors. He was furious, of course. He probably considered shooting me with his pistol, but in the end he decided to murder me indirectly by—"

"By arranging for your conscription," I said. "Janowitz the innkeeper told me."

"I was sent to a training camp in Düsseldorf, where they taught me how to use a bayonet—never above the waist, or the blade might get caught in your enemy's ribs, but always a long thrust to the belly, then a short thrust. They put our battalion on a train to Kleinbrück. I was the only private on board who knew what our officers had in mind. By hiding in the lavatory of a passenger coach, I avoided being frog-marched past the painting."

"A narrow escape," said Ilona.

"According to my superiors, I fought bravely during the Frontiers campaign," said Werner, "so they made me a sergeant, then a lieutenant. When I got to the Marne, I started hearing about a syndrome called shell-shock, and how the victims were normally sent to Träumenchen for treatment. So I began calling myself Viktor Zimmer and pretended the guns and the bombs had made me crazy. Anything to get back inside this place so I could try to foil Herr Direktor."

"An ingenious scheme," said Ilona.

Werner seized the carafe and poured himself a second cup of coffee. "Your turpentine attack was bound to fail, Francis, but I'm pleased to infer you've grasped the necessity of fighting Caligari."

"Is it possible the crimson curtain makes the painting blind?" asked Ilona. "Could we take an ax and murder it through the velvet?"

"The beast would outmaneuver us," said Werner.

"Perhaps we should give the turpentine strategy another chance," I said. "I'm imagining a coordinated strike by you, me, Ilona, and Conrad."

"Please try to understand: we're up against black magic here, not the Three Musketeers," said Werner. "Any merely physical assault is doomed from the outset. We can battle Caligari's sorcery only with sorcery of our own."

"Very well, but I'm no sorcerer," I said.

"Neither am I."

"Nor am I," said Ilona.

Werner rose from the parallelogram table and approached the Spider Queen. He cupped her jaw in his palms, pressed his fingers against her cheeks, and looked her in the eye. "Ilona, my dear, that is not entirely true." Gently he turned her face toward mine. "When I was Fräulein Wessels's art therapist, I observed qualities in her that she herself did not perceive."

"I'm a lunatic, not a witch," she said.

"What you are, Ilona Wessels," said Werner, sliding his hands from her cheeks, "is an artist of infinite potential."

"Please don't use that word," said Ilona.

" 'Artist'?"

" 'Infinite.' I'll explain later."

"Let me lay all my cards on the table," said Werner. "I don't simply want to sabotage Caligari's Kriegsmaschine. I want to replace it with a Friedensmaschine."

"A *peace* machine?" I said.

"After what I saw on the Frontiers and the Marne, all that absurd slaughter, I won't rest until we've taken down *Verzückte Weisheit* and substituted another magical work of art—the antiwar painting to end all antiwar paintings."

"I think I should have stayed in America," I said,

heaving a sigh. "All this Continental esoterica is beyond me."

"Herr Slevoght, I could never make a picture such as you have in mind," said Ilona.

"Do you know why I made a secret copy of the museum key?" Werner asked. "So I could visit your spiderwebs whenever I wished, even in the middle of the night." He took his coffee cup in hand and slowly orbited the table. "On Sunday morning at ten o'clock we three shall gather in the gallery, so that Francis might experience the full magnitude of your gifts. Where is the key now?"

"Under a loose floorboard in the sitting room," said Ilona. "I have no gifts. These days I am a theory person."

Werner explained that before our next meeting he and Conrad would scour the subterranean atelier for materials that might aid our project. I supplied him with the key, then cast my mind ahead to Sunday. The thought of once again entering the vicinity of *Ecstatic Wisdom* terrified me, and yet I felt duty-bound to help counteract the contagion Caligari had unleashed.

"Knock four times, Morse Code for H." Werner set down his cup, then pulled the red bandana from his pocket. "Heaven, hell, hope, horror—take your pick."

"Truth to tell, Herr Slevoght, I wish you'd never returned," said Ilona as she and I escorted him into the foyer. "I wish you and Conrad had taken a cottage on the Rhine."

Werner restored the disguise to his mouth and nose. "Believe me, Fräulein, I hate being the bearer of bad news and worse obligations." He opened the door and stepped into the corridor. "And yet I fear that the destiny of regiments lies in your enchanted hands."

Ilona fixed on her hands, and she was still staring at them long after Werner had gone.

On Sunday morning Ilona and I arrived outside the museum at the appointed hour. I knocked in the prearranged rhythm. Still dressed in his threadbare uniform, Werner admitted us. Sucking on an unlit cigarette, Conrad slouched in the far corner, within arm's reach of *Ecstatic Wisdom*, which was once again masked in velvet.

"*Guten Morgen*, Herr Röhrig," said Ilona.

"I'm happy to see you have taken our side," I said.

"I shall never carry water for Caligari again," said Conrad, lighting his cigarette.

Werner sidled toward the spiderweb oils, then turned and solicited me with a hooked index finger. "Come, Francis. Observe what our arachnophiliac has wrought."

"I've already seen them," I said.

"No, you haven't."

I approached Ilona's oils and scrutinized the mandala web, the surrounding plaster still bearing the marks of her mallet attack.

"Concentrate on the axis," said Werner. "What do you see?"

"A web and a spider."

"Keep looking."

Suddenly, before my astonished eyes—as if the painting were a Victorian zoetrope frieze or a strip of nickelodeon celluloid—the spider came to life. It abandoned the lower corner of the canvas and crawled north to the center of the web. Now the mandala began to rotate. An instant later a rainbow suffused the threads, turning them carmine, then azure, violet, jade, emerald, turquoise, as if Ilona had modeled her painting on a bejeweled wheel from King Sargon's ceremonial chariot.

"How beautiful," I said.

"*Danke schön*," said Ilona.

"Why didn't you tell me—?"

"That my spiders will sometimes come to life? I thought that fact would frighten you. It frightens me."

The mandala stopped turning, and the painting reverted to its original static form. I shifted my gaze to the suspension bridge. At first the oblong image seemed inert, but then five travelers (homunculi by the scale of the world beyond the picture) came on stage and started crossing an unseen chasm. Abruptly the spider appeared at the end of the span, blocking the party's progress.

"Is she going to murder them?" I asked.

"Never confuse predation with immorality, young Francis."

The drama on the bridge froze. I shifted my focus to the

maelstrom. Although the subject was inherently kinetic, this painted Charybdis was actually spinning, the spider herself riding on the whirlpool's foamy lip. I peered into the funnel. The remains of a sunken city rotated about the black core: towers, turrets, ramparts, bridges—flotsam from a lost civilization, stirred up by the vortex.

"The ruins of Atlantis," I said.

"No, Lyonesse," said Ilona as the maelstrom become a mere spiderweb again.

"Outwardly your masterpiece will look exactly like *Ecstatic Wisdom*, an illusion you'll create by replicating Caligari's epic on a linen scrim. That way we can substitute one painting for the other without arousing suspicion. But beneath the surface of the facsimile, waiting to emerge and beguile the troops, will lie a panorama as potent as anything our wicked magician ever wrought."

"Herr Slevoght, you should not imagine I can command my talents. Most of the paintings I made for you have no magic in them. They're dead as timestones."

"Tombstones," said Werner.

I turned away from Ilona's webs and, approaching Werner, asked him how the hunt in the atelier had gone. He reported discovering the preliminary pieces Caligari had made for *Ecstatic Wisdom*, nine charcoal sketches and eleven watercolors that would "guide Ilona when she paints the facsimile on the scrim." Conrad had secured these studies in his apartments along with the other fruits of the morning's quest: Caligari's original brushes, his pair of oversized easels, and four mahogany bars he'd evidently set aside "to remount the canvas if damp weather ever warped the original stretcher frame." As for the beakers of ensorcelled paint, Werner had found these sealed with wax discs and locked away in a cabinet. The pigments themselves were caked and dried, "but careful applications of linseed oil may resuscitate them." When I told Werner about the outré ingredients I'd seen Caligari dissolving in his potions—salamander, beetle, toad, slug, bird embryos—he hypothesized that "their powers are probably still bound to the pigments, but we'll let our Spider Queen be the judge of that."

Ilona marched across the gallery and fixed on the maelstrom web. "I keep thinking about the regiments. Those poor doomed schoolboys and their timestones."

"You can save them," said Werner.

She shifted her attention to the mandala. A thick silence enshrouded the gallery.

"I'm going to need an enormous canvas," she said.

"Of course," said Werner.

"Cut and stretched to the precise dimensions of *Ecstatic Wisdom*."

"I still have the sideshow tent Caligari and I carted around the countryside," said Conrad. "I shall gladly sacrifice it."

"And an equally large scrim for the forgery," said Ilona.

"The infirmary has many yards of linen bandages,"

said Conrad.

Ilona closed her eyes. "An audacious idea is forming in my brain—a plan by which I might gain control of my abilities."

"Tell us," said Werner.

"On the staff of this place are a half-dozen hypnotists." She opened her eyes. "If somebody were to put me in a trance—not a depleting trance, not what Svengali did to Trilby, but a nourishing trance—then maybe . . . do you grasp my reasoning?"

"As it happens, there is one such hypnotist in this very room," said Conrad. "Years ago, while portraying Caligari's somnambulist, I absorbed the fundamentals of mesmerism."

"I have a title in mind for my picture," said Ilona. "*The Corpse Factory of Dr. Caligari.*"

"That sounds like an act rejected by Le Grand Guignol," I said.

"How about *Totentanz*?" said Ilona.

"I like that," said Werner.

"Myself as well," said Conrad.

"What does it mean?" I asked.

"The dance of the dead," said Ilona.

In the days that followed, she became a force of nature and a wonder to behold, every atom of her being fixed on the needs of *Totentanz*. Were she not an atheist, I imagine she would have prayed. Were she given to mystical visions, she might have fasted. Instead she sat for hours at the dining room table, alternately drinking coffee and brandy, all the while filling a sketchbook with incomprehensible charcoal drawings that I took to be preliminary studies for her imminent epic.

Throughout this interval I continued to teach presumably therapeutic art lessons. Ilona attended my classes intermittently, as did Werner—much to the delight and perplexity of his former students. When Gaston, Ludwig, and Pietro swore to keep Leutnant Zimmer's true identity a secret, Werner and I elected to take them at their word (they were crazy, not dishonest), and all three lunatics offered equally sincere vows of silence after we recruited them into our plot against Caligari. True, they didn't entirely grasp our larger political agenda, but they understood that we'd accorded them the honor of membership in a conspiracy.

"Think of it as a kind of game," I told them.

"There is only one game," said our Grandmaster, "but I shall be pleased to help Ilona make a magic picture."

"I shall likewise lend my courage and fortitude to this daring mission," said Ludwig. "We officers in Die Erste Galaxisbrigade live by a code."

"I always knew Caligari was my enemy," said Pietro. "Of course, everyone is my enemy, but some of you are more ready than others to pour honey down my throat and release the ants."

On the last day in September, much to my horror, Ilona seized a pair of scissors and cut her hair almost down to the scalp, so that, once the composition process began, her tresses wouldn't trail across the palette, mushing blobs of pigment together. When I first beheld my shorn Spider Queen, I gasped in dismay, but by the end of the week I'd decided she was as comely as ever—more so, actually, in a Nefertiti sort of way.

Twenty-four hours later I presented our Grandmaster, our space traveler, and our paranoid with a reel of measuring tape from my supply cabinet, then supervised them as, working in Conrad's gas-lit back parlor, they sliced a huge segment, 9 meters long by 4.5 meters high, out of the sideshow tent. The following day I had the students sneak the block of canvas, the oversized easels, and the mahogany bars into my sitting room (I'd already removed the standard easel and a dozen nonpictorial paintings, stashing them in the bedroom closet). By the light washing through the casement, our lunatics screwed the bars together into a stretcher frame congruent with *Ecstatic Wisdom*, affixed the canvas to the wood with carpet tacks, and tightened it further by moistening the reverse side. They primed the obverse with gesso using a brush so broad it could have painted a barn.

Meanwhile Ilona set about analyzing Caligari's cryptic pigments. After Conrad brought her the beakers, she removed the wax seals and irrigated each color—vermilion, cadmium yellow, viridian, ultramarine—using a pipette filled with linseed oil. On instructions from Ilona, Conrad transferred the restored paints to ceramic mustard pots. Taking up the vermilion, she inserted her index finger until it contacted the paint. She held the sample up to the light, inspecting it with a skeptical eye. She sniffed the smear. She tasted it. She brought the pot to her ear and listened. I thought she was about to reveal the results of her analysis, but instead she submitted the remaining pots to the same sensory tests.

"We are fortunate," she declared at last, exhibiting her guileless but knowing smile. "Caligari's powers still inhabit these mixtures. The catalytic agents—salamander, beetle, toad, slug, unhatched birds—remain active and need not be reintroduced. Even the incantations have survived. *Effundam spiritum meum in vobis, virtutibus. Perfectus es.*"

Throughout the first two weeks in October, inspired by the stolen sketches and watercolors, Ilona channeled her energies toward creating the counterfeit *Ecstatic Wisdom* beneath which *Totentanz* would lie camouflaged. Hour by hour, working on the floor of the sitting room, she applied the potions to the immense linen scrim Werner and I had sewn together from stolen bandages. Every time I glanced at the emerging forgery, the more confident I became that our scheme would succeed, for it was the very Doppelgänger of Caligari's magnum opus.

When not busy preparing the facsimile, Ilona joined Conrad in his apartments, and together they pursued their hypnotism experiments. During each session Conrad invited his subject to contemplate alternately a rotating wheel of multicolored glass and a phosphorescent spiral painted on a spinning disc. As these two entrancing moons bore Ilona to the shores of an uncommon sleep, Conrad offered exhortations of the sort declaimed by the anonymous narrator of Mr. Edgar Allan Poe's "The Facts in the Case of M. Valdemar." Nine trances later Ilona and Conrad had little to show for their collaboration, but she remained optimistic.

"It's simply a matter of time," she said.

On the Ides of October Ilona instructed me to comb through the asylum library seeking books containing military photographs and drawings. Pictures of technical innovations—flamethrowers, machine guns, howitzers, Minenwerfers, dirigibles—would be particularly useful, she said, likewise medical illustrations depicting the antagonistic and lopsided relationship between war and flesh. My mission proved successful, supplying her with a plentitude of abhorrent images.

As an All Saints Day sun rose over Weizenstaat, an exhilarated Conrad summoned Werner and me to the dining room, where Ilona stood beside the table holding her sketchbook open to a drawing of an infantryman snarled in barbed wire.

"The hypnotism has done what we'd hoped," she said. "My talents are now fully my own."

"Look closely," said Conrad. "This will amaze you."

The pen-and-ink infantryman moved, actually moved,

convulsing and retching inside his fanged prison, as if his ordeal had been recorded on frames of motion-picture film now unspooling through a kinematograph. The barbed wire vibrated with his anguished spasms. I could hear his cries of despair.

Ilona flipped to another drawing. A bugler writhed in a field of poppies, his left hand holding his tarnished instrument, both his legs amputated by an artillery shell. Although her medium was black ink, a bright red fluid leaked from the stumps, ran to the edge of the page, and stained the table.

Now that she had recovered and bridled her gifts (for the immediate future at least), Ilona threw herself into the creation of *Totentanz*. Using the sitting room floor as a drawing board, she prepared a full-scale study for the entire painting, sketching the contours and textures on a huge grid she'd patched together from a hundred sheets of asylum stationery. The scene centered on a figure she'd named "Korporal Hans Jedermann"—Corporal John Everyman—a clean-shaven, baby-faced, all-purpose soldier dressed in a nondescript brown uniform and fearfully surveying a no-man's-land sprawling between the trenches of opposing armies.

Availing herself of calipers, graphite sticks, and gum erasers, Ilona stood before the stretcher frame and began copying the *Totentanz* study onto the dried gesso. She permitted Werner and me to assist her, confident we would replicate her drawing precisely. The project consumed an entire week. Our lines were ephemeral and delicate, so the pigments could cover them like jam on bread.

On the first Sunday in November, while men fought and died in the Battle of Armentières (one of a dozen hideously indecisive sequels to the Marne), Ilona solemnly presented herself to the canvas, a palette in one hand, a pig-bristle brush in the other, and applied a supernatural dab of vermilion. The great work had begun. As the month elapsed, she labored around the clock, pausing only for brief naps and modest portions of bread, cheese, fruit, and wine. At her insistence Conrad stole a phial of cocaine from the asylum's pharmaceutical supplies, but before taking up the syringe she decided that the project itself was the only euphoriant she needed.

Twenty-four hours after the first snows of December had blanketed the asylum, Ilona invited our cabal into the sitting room.

"It's not quite dry," she said. "No fingers."

Cautiously I approached the stretcher frame. A familiar image displayed itself: Caligari's epic—that is, Ilona's forgery of Caligari's epic—with its happy schoolboys marching off to war. Now *Totentanz* took command of the linen scrim, and the nearest *Ecstatic Wisdom* soldier looked me in the eye and gave me to know his thoughts.

*I no longer work for the generals, friend, nor for the princes, but you must not tell them that. Please allow my brother-in-arms Korporal Jedermann to show you an edifying panorama painted by Ilona Wessels, Europe's greatest living artist.*

In thrall to the magic canvas, the scrim became as transparent as cellophane, and *Totentanz* shone through. There was Hans Jodermann, rifle on his shoulder, casting his bewildered gaze across the battleground. The painting resolved into a succession of discrete tableaux. Soldiers hoisted themselves free of their trenches only to meet the sweeping scythe of massed rifle fire, a quick and mechanized harvest that soon littered no-man's-land with corpses. Several youths were cut in two, actually cut in two, by the saber-sharp efficiency of the machine guns. Artillery rained shells on charging battalions, the explosions launching severed limbs in all directions like embers flying free of a bonfire. My skull reverberated with bugles bleating, drums thundering, grenades detonating, cannons convulsing, horses neighing in terror, wounded soldiers screaming for their mothers.

"This will bring entire armies to their senses," said Conrad.

"It's the Marne—it's the Marne, and you weren't even *there*," said Werner. "Fräulein, you are a marvel."

"A marvel, a genius, and—I don't doubt it—Europe's greatest living artist," I said, even as I gagged on the air around the stretcher frame, a miasma of cordite, vomitus, fear, feces, burned flesh, and the iron odor of blood.

"This morning I woke up with a headache, and that means brain cancer," said Pietro.

"Vicious as they can be, when Ganymedians go to war, it is never this bad," said Ludwig.

"Check and mate," said Gaston.

"Well played, Dr. Caligari," said Conrad, "but you lost."

"It occurs to me that a day may come when I shall need to restore a damaged section of *Totentanz*," said Ilona. "We must hide the pigments where Herr Doktor will never find them."

Conrad said, "I'll wrap each pot in cheesecloth, put all four in a waterproof case, and bury them—"

"Beneath the sundial in the courtyard," said Ilona.

"Done and done," said Conrad.

Again I scanned her masterpiece. It was indeed the antiwar painting to end all antiwar paintings. It was perhaps even the antiwar painting to end war itself. Were someone to carve on my tombstone—or, as Ilona would have it, my timestone—a simple six-word epitaph, ASSISTED IN THE CREATION OF TOTENTANZ, that would be good enough for me.

# FOUR

Shortly after dawn on Friday the 25th of December, 1914, feeling confident that even Alessandro Caligari would not consider Christmas morning an appropriate time for war profiteering, we peeled the linen *Ecstatic Wisdom* forgery from Ilona's painting, detached *Totentanz* from the mahogany bars, disassembled the stretcher frame, and rolled up the dried canvas like a rug. We bore the components of our conspiracy down the passageway to the museum door, then cautiously admitted ourselves. The gallery was blessedly deserted. As always, Herr Direktor's magnum opus—at the moment mantled in velvet—commanded the west wall. We laid our materials beneath Ilona's spiderweb oils, then set about making the grand substitution.

Gaston, Ludwig, Pietro, and I took *Ecstatic Wisdom* in hand, grasping the bottom edge and lifting the suspension cable clear of the three spikes. We staggered backward under the weight of the stretcher frame. I half expected the painting to harm us in some way, perhaps by transforming its pigments into chlorine gas or its cable into a poisonous snake, but we conveyed it to the elevator hatch without mishap, resting it vertically on the platform.

Werner approached the winch and began turning the crank as if operating an immense coffee grinder. With a harsh screeching of pulleys and a strident clattering of chains, the platform descended, delivering the malign painting, the lunatics, and myself into the depths of the cellar. Taking care not to smash any of Caligari's alchemical apparatus, we slid *Ecstatic Wisdom* across the length of the atelier, the mahogany bar functioning like the runner on a sled, and secluded it in a cavernous alcove.

There remained the task of retrieving the crimson curtain. Apprehensive that the monster might awaken, I grasped the material with both hands and slowly lifted it free of the canvas. Although I heard faint whisperings of "La Marseillaise," *Ecstatic Wisdom* remained otherwise inert, evidently oblivious to our presence. We exited the alcove, then folded the curtain into a rectangle the size of a coffin lid. Embracing the velvet pile, I led the students back to the elevator platform.

Werner worked the winch. As soon as the gallery floor was whole again, I set the curtain in the corner, even as Gaston, Ludwig, and Pietro began reconstructing *Totentanz*. It took them a mere half-hour to assemble the frame, affix the canvas, and screw the cable in place. Assisted by Conrad, they carried Ilona's *chef d'oeuvre* to the west wall and hung it on the spikes.

Acting on an unspoken consensus, we arrayed ourselves before our peace machine, until the maimings and the pain, the thundering guns and the bursting shells, became too much for us to bear, and we turned away.

"*Consurge, daemon!*" cried Ilona, gesturing toward the *Ecstatic Wisdom* forgery. Like a lethargic phantom, the scrim rose slowly from the floor. "*Vola!*" It floated toward the west wall. "*Vola!*"

The scrim pressed itself against the canvas and, surrendering to the power of *Totentanz*, became sufficiently opaque to camouflage the canvas. Our Grandmaster, space traveler, and paranoid retrieved the velvet curtain, straightaway draping it over the stretcher frame.

"Together we have written a new and shining chapter in the history of Western art," said Werner.

"And a new and shining chapter in the history of Western ethics," I said. "The sleep of reason breeds monsters. The light of knowledge breeds gods."

"Perhaps," said Conrad. "And yet I fear the ink is not yet dry on our new and shining chapters. There is still time for Caligari to smear the pages."

Energized by hope, hobbled by anxiety, Ilona, Werner, Conrad, and I stepped onto the parapet overlooking the Moselle River footbridge. It was Saturday morning, the 26th of December. Hoarfrost glazed the sedge-covered hills. The bell in the clock tower tolled seven times, the last two peals melding with the shriek of a locomotive whistle.

"Herr Direktor is back in business," said Conrad, focusing his field glasses on the train station.

"In England they call this Boxing Day," I said. "From now until sunset, the wealthy will give Christmas parcels to servants and tradespeople."

"During the Marne, every day was Boxing Day," said Werner. "We crated up whatever was left of Karl or Herman or Rudolf and sent it to Division Headquarters."

The troop train rolled onto a siding, brakes squealing, boiler chuffing, and an instant later a column of unarmed German recruits came pouring from the coaches like Achaeans exiting the Trojan horse. Goaded by their superior officers, they headed for the footbridge.

"The *Berliner Morgenpost* publishes deployment timetables, though of course each unit's final destination is censored," said Conrad. "This regiment is part of the newly formed German Fourteenth Corps."

Suddenly Caligari was on the scene, waddling toward the chained oaken doors to the museum, one hand gripping his cane, the other holding a metal key that, struck by the sun, blazed like an Olympic torch. He opened the padlock, allowing the chain to slither to the ground. From his overcoat he produced a second key, then unlocked the museum doors and disappeared into the gallery.

"We have nothing to fear," I said, struggling to believe

myself. "The forgery is flawless."

"Only God is flawless," said Ilona. "It's the first thing you'll notice about Him if he ever gets around to existing."

Caligari returned to daylight, having evidently raised the curtain on *Totentanz* in its *Ecstatic Wisdom* disguise. His placid countenance suggested that he'd detected nothing untoward. An instant later the recruits began entering the museum, there to experience Ilona's sorcery as the scrim, shedding its opacity at the bidding of *Totentanz*, became a window on the Devil's backyard.

I borrowed the field glasses, then studied the first half-dozen soldiers to exit the gallery. Determined not to betray the conspiracy into which the painted but loquacious Hans Jedermann had drawn them (my angst was quickly turning to optimism), each man had worked his face into a credible facsimile of Kriegslust, even as his gait became a persuasive impersonation of Soldatentum. Did Caligari realize that today's patrons were merely feigning bellicosity? If so, his demeanor revealed no sign of suspicion or alarm.

"Ilona's magic is working," I insisted, passing the field glasses to Werner. "Her genius is equal to Caligari's."

"When this war is over," said Ilona, "I shall allow the Louvre to acquire my painting."

"How do we label the condition of these men?" said Werner, training the glasses on the museum doors. "What is the opposite of shell-shocked?"

"Truth-struck?" I suggested.

Conrad nodded in assent. "Very good, Francis. Castration by barbed wire is a reality not easily denied. Nothing could be more factual than dismemberment by a grenade."

Occasionally, on leaving the gallery, a private, corporal, or sergeant would lift his head toward the parapet and stare at Ilona, his gaze betraying admiration shading into adoration.

*Perhaps this benign witch has not shown me the way home, but she has turned me from the path of annihilation.*

"They sense you are the artist," said Werner.

"These schoolboys are your children," I said.

"And after he bids farewell to his trench," said Ilona, "if any soldier needs a letter of transit signed by his mother, I shall be happy to provide it."

Four more trains arrived that day, so that by sunset the rest of the German XIV Corps, 3rd Regiment, most of the French XI Corps, 5th Regiment, and at least six hundred reservists from the British Expeditionary Force had seen the war through Hans Jedermann's eyes.

Although it was too early for reports concerning mysterious outbreaks of pacifism in the trenches, I carefully scrutinized the next day's *New York Herald*, learning more than I wanted to know about the Battle of Artois (an offensive through which Marshal Joffre hoped to discourage General Falkenhayn from sending divisions off to fight

France's valued ally, Russia, on the Eastern Front). The next four editions of the *Herald* likewise provided no clues to the efficacy of *Totentanz*. But then came the issue of Friday the 3rd of January, 1915, proclaiming an event that for Ilona, Werner, Conrad, and myself would admit of but one explanation.

MASSIVE DESERTIONS ON WESTERN FRONT, shouted the headline. THOUSANDS OF GERMAN, FRENCH, BRITISH SOLDIERS SEEK SANCTUARY IN NONALIGNED NATIONS, ran the subhead. The story corroborated our explanation in full, for the fleeing troops belonged to the very regiments whose psyches we'd massaged on the day after Christmas. Among the many soldiers who'd sought and found refuge in neutral Holland to the north, neutral Weizenstaat to the east, and neutral Switzerland to the south, several had given *Herald* correspondents thoughtful (if rather baroque) accounts of their conversions.

"This isn't a war, it's a cabaret act staged by Mephistopheles," a German corporal opined.

"Our lieutenants and captains are honorable men, but our generals spend their days spreading horse manure on a garden of delusions," a French private asserted.

"And meanwhile the ruling elites sit around in Paris and Berlin," a German sergeant added, "sipping rosé and schnapps and devising clever reasons why the slaughter must continue."

"My heart is courageous, but my intestines are finicky,"

a British Tommy explained. "They refuse to be spindled around a bayonet."

In mid-January our pacifist insurrection hit a snag when armed patrols deployed by Holland, Weizenstaat, and Switzerland started detaining fugitive soldiers at their respective borders, there being a limit to how many hot-eyed armistice addicts these circumspect nations were willing to absorb. Meanwhile, military police from the armies of Marshal Joffre, General Falkenhayn, and General Haig had started tracking down deserters, alternately throwing them into prison and shooting them on sight.

And yet the great *Totentanz* revolt continued, for as winter progressed the deserters learned how to lose their pursuers in the frozen depths of swamps and woodlands. Defying the harsh weather, galvanized by their newfound political principles, these roving bands of pacifists appropriated the Ardennes and the Schwarzwald like Robin Hood and his Merrie Men camping out in Sherwood Forest. While hunger was not unknown among Ilona's children, most managed to feed themselves by poaching, fishing, foraging, plundering henhouses, and eliciting civilian acts of charity at gunpoint.

The longer *Totentanz* continued to occasion vacancies on the Western Front, the more vulnerable we all felt to detection by Caligari. As a logical precaution, Conrad kept his distance from the rest of us. And while Werner continued to attend my art classes in the guise of Leutnant Zimmer, he otherwise eschewed the company of Ilona and myself.

Among us four conspirators, it was the Spider Queen who proved the most sensitive to the moral ambiguities inherent in our scheme. "To be honest," she told me, "there are times when I imagine us taking down *Totentanz* and restoring the real *Ecstatic Wisdom*, leaving Caligari none the wiser."

"Taking it down?" I said, attempting to sound perplexed, although in fact I knew exactly what she meant.

"By shaping the souls of unsuspecting schoolboys, are we not indulging in a species of hubris as monstrous as Caligari's?"

It was Saint Valentine's Day. The big news from the forward lines was the Battle of Champagne, whose masterminds had arranged the sanguinary irrigation of a terrain normally devoted to growing grapes for wine.

"I understand your distress, Ilona," I said. "But let's remember we've delivered thousands of soldiers on both sides from untimely deaths."

"And yet we must ask ourselves: do those saved lives belong entirely to the young men who are living them—or have we simply replaced Caligari's sleepwalkers with puppets of our own? I have no answer, young Francis, and neither does Conrad or Werner, and neither do you."

Later that afternoon we tried to lose ourselves in one of our collaborative painting sessions. Standing shoulder to shoulder before the easel, we grasped our mutual camel's-hair brush and directed it toward a stretched canvas to which we'd applied a slate-blue undercoat.

"When I agreed to create a peace machine for Herr Slevoght," said Ilona, "I assumed we would soon pump so many pacifists into this war that all the divisions would become unglued and an armistice would follow. Now we know military justice will catch up with most of those same pacifists. Every time I read that a deserter has been shot, I want to throw myself out a window."

"I know the feeling well," I said as a scarlet lightning bolt appeared on the blue field. Evidently our collective psyche was in an Expressionist mood. "The impulse always passes. I'm not sure why, but it does."

"Young Francis, we must vow to subtract all windows from our lives, likewise pistols, ropes, and shaving razors."

Together we superimposed a scarlet heart on the lightning bolt. "Happy Valentine's Day," I said.

"Were it not for *la cura amore*," said Ilona, "I would have gone insane by now."

Throughout the rest of February and well into March, the chronic Battle of Champagne played out in a roundelay of feeble assaults and ineffectual counterassaults. Marshal Joffre's regiments would compliantly advance, then fall back, then stoically advance, then fall back, then advance, then fall back, each sputtering engagement more futile than the one before. Taking note of all these Sisyphean theatrics, Sir John French decided that a full-bore attack was required. The English general's plan called for a division of the British IV Corps and two regiments of the Indian Corps to aim their artillery at a crucial sector of no-man's-land, sweeping it free of barbed wire with surprise barrages, then drive General Falkenhayn's troops out of their trenches with grenades before reinforcements could arrive. As the *pièce de résistance*, the British and Indians would take the village of Neuve Chapelle back from the Germans, who were rumored to have secluded a secret weapon in the nearby Bois du Biez prior to testing it in battle.

From my perspective the most significant event of Wednesday the 10th of March, 1915, was not the start of the Battle of Neuve Chapelle—indeed, only after the fact did I learn of Marshal French's decision to launch an offensive on that date—but rather a message from Conrad stating that, twenty-four hours hence, Dr. Caligari expected Ilona and me to join him for coffee in his office. My lover and I found Herr Direktor's summons ominous in the extreme. Having finally discovered the peace machine (or so we assumed), he intended to hand us over to some international tribunal or other, so that the justices could execute us for conspiring to deprive the generals and princes of their absolutely marvelous and entirely terrific war.

Taking deep breaths, mimicking the carriage of an innocent man, I strode into Caligari's salon, Ilona right behind me. Our host occupied a plush burgundy sofa. Two strapping bodyguards, one tall, the other taller, both dressed anachronistically in the ornate uniforms of Turkish janissaries, stood with folded arms beside a low teakwood table holding a silver coffee service and a plate of cakes and strudels. Speaking not a word, Caligari gestured us into a pair of fine leather chairs, whereupon the taller janissary filled two porcelain cups with a coffee whose fragrance hinted of a Viennese heritage.

"This is the first time I've ever permitted a lunatic in my office," said Caligari.

"Might I suggest that the term 'lunatic' is not useful in Ilona's case?" I said. "I'm not convinced it's useful in anybody's case."

"Who wants cake?" asked the shorter janissary.

Ilona and I mumbled in the affirmative, and the bodyguard got to work.

"Dr. Verguin no longer believes Fräulein Wessels's spider fixation portends a psychotic break," said Caligari. "In our medical director's view, Ilona's arachnophilia is completely cured. What is your opinion, Mr. Wyndham?"

"Speaking as Ilona's art therapist, I'm willing to let her walk free of Träumenchen," I said, taking a large swallow of splendid coffee. "Speaking as her *inamorato*—"

"It would be foolish to discharge me," said Ilona. "I'm still the Spider Queen of Ogygia."

"If you were truly mad, you wouldn't know it,"

said Caligari.

"Then I'm the Spider Queen of Ogygia, and I don't know it."

"You are Ilona Wessels of Holstenwall. I shall instruct Nurse Roussel to prepare the paperwork."

"I'm not yet ready to leave," said Ilona, sipping coffee.

"This is a mental institution, Fräulein, not a boarding house." Caligari turned and waggled a silver spoon in my face. "How are your other students faring?"

"Ludwig Ruttluff is planning a flight to Neptune," I said, finishing my coffee. "Pietro Barbieri still suffers from pantophobia. Gaston Duchemin remains an eternal spectator at Paulsen versus Morphy."

"What about Viktor Zimmer?"

"Shell-shock cases are always challenging, but I do see improvement."

"I have a suggestion regarding Leutnant Zimmer. Why not restore his real name to him? Why not call him Werner Slevoght?"

"I don't know what you mean," I said, nausea surging through my digestive tract.

"*She* knows what I mean." Caligari jabbed the silver spoon in Ilona's direction. "Was it not Slevoght who persuaded you to paint an embarrassingly moralistic picture and conceal it beneath a forgery of *Ecstatic Wisdom*?"

Ilona grimaced and closed her eyes. "I miss Herr Slevoght," she said at last, "who was nearly Francis's equal as a painting master, but I do not fantasize that he has returned. Last month I dreamed he'd died in the Battle of the Marne. These visions of mine are often pathetic."

"Prophetic," I said, reeling with dread. "If Pietro's condition were contagious, Signore, I would say you've contracted a touch of paranoia. I might even hypothesize—"

My tongue seized up, went numb, became a dead snail in my mouth. Seeking to clear my mind, I lurched out of my chair. My knees buckled, and I collapsed on the Persian rug as, one by one, the candles of my brain guttered out.

After an indeterminate interval I awoke, dazed, queasy, and lying on my back. My skull reverberated as if enduring an artillery barrage, though the cause was surely whatever drug Caligari had put in the coffee. A grid of iron bars hovered before my gaze, each interstice the size of a hopscotch square: the ceiling of a cage, I speculated—a theory I confirmed by standing up and apprehending to my dismay that four additional grids surrounded me. I was not alone in the cube. A dazed Ilona stood in the far corner, flanked by Werner and Conrad. The astringent odor of oil pigments told me we were in Caligari's underground atelier.

"Our peace machine stayed in operation much longer than I would have predicted," muttered Werner.

"Caligari told me we were betrayed by his cat," said Conrad. "Our mystic went looking for his lost Cesare down here and happened upon his magnum opus hidden in the alcove."

The alienist sat outside the cage on a wooden stool, the seat creaking beneath his considerable rump. He was paring his fingernails. I saw no sign of whomever had helped him imprison us, but I assumed his Turkish soldiers had done the deed.

"You'll be pleased to hear you occupy a privileged vantage, front row seats at a spectacle of great political and aesthetic significance." With his cane Caligari directed our attention to an immense rectangular object propped against a workbench and draped with two bed-sheets pinned together to form a white curtain. "Leutnant Slevoght, allow me to applaud your ingenuity. For several months you managed to beat me at my own game." He grasped the white curtain and yanked it away. Below lay Ilona's duplicate of his epic, its war-loving schoolboys momentarily obscuring her own panorama. "As for the real *Ecstatic Wisdom*, it's back where it belongs. Listen carefully, and you'll hear the tramping of boots and the singing of anthems. By this time tomorrow, a platoon of my janissaries will be guarding it around the clock."

Caligari rose and disappeared into the shadows, returning straightaway with a cylinder strapped to his back: a 1.2 meter Fiedler flamethrower—I recognized it from my *Totentanz* research—complete with fuel supply, rubber hose, and steel nozzle. He ripped the linen scrim away, revealing

Ilona's picture, then flung the fabric into the air. As the counterfeit painting floated on an updraft, he aimed the nozzle and depressed the lever, causing the propellant gas to drive a stream of flammable oil through the hose and across the burning wick. A jet of fire leapt from the nozzle and struck the scrim, instantly reducing it to smoking threads of carbonized fabric.

"Thus to all forgeries!"

He released the lever, and the shaft of flame vanished, even as the fire, bereft of fuel, went out. From the pocket of his trousers he produced his pistol, setting it on the stool.

"Do I intend to incinerate the four of you as well? A tempting notion, but I believe I'll shoot you instead, lest you think me some cruel ecclesiastic sending witches to die in agony at the stake. But first comes the main event, the long overdue immolation of . . . does your impertinent painting have a name, Fräulein?"

"*Totentanz*," said Ilona. "Be warned. It knows how to protect itself."

Was she bluffing? I wasn't sure, but in any event Caligari's next remark rendered the question moot.

"If the oil in this cylinder were of an ordinary provenance, it would indeed be reckless of me to attack your picture. But I brewed it here in my laboratory, and you know what *that* means."

He inserted a fresh igniter into the nozzle (taking care not to burn his fingers on the hot steel), then lit the wick with a wooden match. He took aim, depressed the lever, and sent forth a spew of fiery vomit. It struck the upper left corner of Ilona's painting, obliterating a vignette of a military dirigible floating over the battlefield.

*"Nein!"* she cried

Caligari released the lever, then inserted and lit a fresh igniter. He fired his weapon. A lick of flame struck the lower right corner of the canvas, destroying a machine-gun nest.

"No!" I screamed as the sickly sweet fragrance of burning pigment filled my nostrils.

*"Fick dich!"* shouted Werner.

The alienist released the lever.

Slowly, inexorably, the ravenous fires inched toward the painting's core, emitting orange embers and black smoke. Everyone coughed, including the alienist. The conflagration boasted an embarrassment of combustibles: pigment, hemp fiber, linseed oil, the wood of the stretcher frame.

Caligari shrugged the flamethrower off his back and removed the pistol from the stool. I did not doubt that he intended to murder us.

There now occurred an event that, even by the irrational norms of Träumenchen, could only be called uncanny. Ignoring the hungry flames devouring *Totentanz*, its central figure, Hans Jedermann, marched free of the burning canvas and strode into the museum cellar. Caligari, startled, jumped backward. The Korporal slid a hand under the strap of his rifle and levered it free of his shoulder. For a fleeting instant he considered shooting Caligari—I could read that intention in his grim lips and narrowed eyes—but instead he pursued a nobler purpose.

"Stand aside!" he insisted in a voice barely accustomed to the timbre of manhood.

With a single shot he blasted the lock off the cage, then yanked back the door. As my colleagues and I stumbled into the cellar, Hans Jedermann seized the abandoned flamethrower and delivered it into Werner's keeping. The Leutnant shouldered the weapon, the cylinder protruding from his spine like Quasimodo's hump. We all knew what must happen now. The Korporal took my hand, then I took Ilona's hand, then Ilona took Conrad's hand. Listing under the weight of the flamethrower, Werner brought up the rear of our procession.

"My dear Fräulein Wessels, here you are in the flesh," said Hans in reverent tones. "You can't imagine the thrill."

"Where are we going?" she asked.

"The Western Front."

"I've been there," said Werner. "How about Barcelona instead?"

"The painting is a portal, not a tram," our John Everyman explained. "I must return whence I came."

As a dumbfounded Caligari escaped up the staircase to the gallery, I allowed Hans to lead me into the doomed painting, the smoke stinging my eyes, the flames singeing my clothes. I passed through the ring of fire, and then

*Totentanz* with its final breath hurled me and my companions from Weizenstaat into northern France . . .

Where we landed supine in a patch of snow beside a swamp. The *Totentanz* stretcher frame loomed over us like the charred and smoldering wall of a fire-gutted barn. Ducks navigated the muddy water in slow circles, unimpressed by our supernatural advent. Darkness crept over the cold March landscape.

Gradually we four conspirators gained our feet, as did the miracle Korporal. I embraced Ilona and said, "I grieve for your great painting."

"I shall make another one day," she said.

Hans directed us toward a gravel road turned silver by the moonlight. For the next half-hour our weary band of wayfarers marched steadily west, Werner stoically carrying the flamethrower. On all sides marsh birds whooped and trilled. Artillery thundered in the distance. Occasionally a flare arced across the sky like a diminutive comet, illuminating the white plain.

"Thus ends day two of the Battle of Neuve Chapelle," said Hans, bringing our little parade to a halt. He unbuckled his canteen, then allowed each of us a swig. "Yesterday morning the British stormed into the village as planned, but God knows if they got as far as the Bois du Biez and the secret weapon. I gather it's a kind of pillbox on motorized treads.

There's a good chance the Germans recaptured Neuve Chapelle today, which means we could conceivably spend the night in a warm hostelry."

"If the Tommies and Falkenhayn's troops are really fighting over some dreadful new killing technology," said Werner, "we should probably stay clear of the village."

"I recommend that we proceed directly to the German line," said Hans. "The sector overseen by my Hauptmann—my captain—near Loos is only one trench deep, but we'll be safe there. He'll receive us graciously, especially when he realizes our party includes includes the woman who painted *Totentanz*." The Korporal strapped the canteen about his waist. "So what sort of man is Hauptmann Pochhammer? The instant I told him I sensed my creator was in trouble, he gave me permission to leave the trenches and rescue you."

Hans went on to explain that, while he was himself "a mere Farbenmensch, a paint person," Pochhammer had made him an honorary member of the VII Corps, 2nd Regiment, 4th Battalion: the Fafnirdrachen Riflemen. Though hardly a pacifist—no commissioned officer of the German Imperial Army could possibly answer to that description—Pochhammer was "an intellectual and contrarian sort of soldier, given to reading poetry and sometimes writing it." So great was his disgust with the way the leaders on all sides "were treating peace feelers like vectors of the plague," Pochhammer had come to regard *Totentanz* as "philosophically superior to *Ecstatic Wisdom*."

"Take us where you will," said Conrad.

"We all owe you our lives," said Ilona.

"True, but I owe you my whole existence, Fräulein," said Hans. "Herr Leutnant, you also played a part in my nativity, as did you, Herr Röhrig, and you, Mr. Wyndham. I know you've had a difficult day, but you must try to stay on your feet for another five kilometers."

We resumed our trek. Within twenty minutes the road disappeared, superseded by an expanse of melting snow spangled with red and yellow wildflowers. We slogged forward. After an hour, we reached the German fortifications. Beyond stretched the scorched and torn earth of no-man's-land, which the periodic flares revealed in all its distressing textures: shell craters, dead horses, black skeletal trees, ferocious matrices of barbed wire. The sentry, an ursine Schütze with a rifle, commanded us to halt.

"At ease, Siegfried," said Hans.

"Did your mission succeed, Herr Korporal?"

Hans gestured toward Ilona. "I saved Fräulein Wessels and, less intentionally, three of her friends."

Entering the trench proved a matter of negotiating a wooden ladder—a skewed and rickety affair, but I was happy to transfer my jeopardized flesh to a subterranean place. Hauptmann Pochhammer personally supervised our descent.

"Fräulein Wessels, I am honored to welcome you to the world of the Fafnirdrachen Riflemen." Pochhammer was a cheery young man with a flourishing moustache and a tightly belted paunch. "Your *Totentanz* has saved many lives."

"It no longer exists," said Ilona.

"How tragic."

"Caligari incinerated it using the enchanted oil in this Flammenwerfer," said Werner, unshouldering the cylinder.

Illuminated by an array of kerosene lanterns, our mudpacked, sandbagged surroundings exuded a peculiar congeniality. The zone occupied by the Fafnirdrachen Riflemen, six hundred and eighty strong, featured three Dutch ovens, a dining area appointed with milking stools and a rectory table, and an elongated dormitory comprising scores of cots and sleeping bags resting on pinewood pallets, but the most refined touch was a private latrine screened by a blanket and well stocked with materials for burying solid waste.

"Let me tell you my idea," said Werner, running his hand along the flamethrower cylinder. "Even though Caligari will never again be careless enough to let anyone mount a pacifist masterpiece in the museum, I can imagine us using this alchemical elixir to cleanse the world of *Verzückte Weisheit* itself."

"Where is the diabolical painting at present?" asked Pochhammer.

"Back on the wall in Kleinbrück," said Werner. "By now Caligari has a gang of mercenaries guarding it. Perhaps, Herr Hauptmann, you would care to donate a platoon to our cause?"

"*Ach*, there's no way to assault the thing in a military action," said Pochhammer. "To do so would violate Weizenstaat's neutrality and make hash of the Hague Conventions."

"So Caligari wins again?" said Ilona, heaving a sigh.

"Don't be sad, Fräulein," said Pochhammer. "For more than ten weeks you and your friends outmaneuvered the sorcerer. The name of Ilona Wessels will appear in all the chronicles of this war."

"I won't be the only lunatic to enjoy such fame," said Ilona. "The men who responded to an isolated act of Slavic terrorism by setting the world on fire will receive a lot of ink as well."

On Pochhammer's invitation we arrayed ourselves around the rectory table. The 4th Battalion's mess officer served us knockwurst on chipped plates, plus Liebfraumilch in tin cups. Our host apologized for the lack of glassware.

"These are impressive accommodations," I remarked.

"Civilization is where you find it," noted Pochhammer. "Sad to say, last week our white linen tablecloth was commandeered for bandages." From his coat pocket he pulled a slender volume of verse by Friedrich Hölderlin. "I find that poetry soothes the digestion."

"Herr Hauptmann, if you would, read us the one about the snakes," said the sandy-haired, loose-limbed Leutnant Afflerbach, and Pochhammer proceeded to oblige him.

*The fruits are ripe, dipped in fire,*
*Cooked and sampled on earth.*
*And there's a law,*
*That things crawl off in the manner of snakes,*
*Prophetically, dreaming on the hills of heaven.*
*And there is much that needs to be retained,*
*Like a load of wood on the shoulders.*
*But the pathways are dangerous.*

Whereupon Werner impressed everyone by supplying the next stanza.

*But what about things that we love?*
*We see sun shining on the ground,*
*and the dry dust,*
*And at home the forests deep with shadows,*
*And smoke flowering from the rooftops,*
*Peacefully, near the ancient crowning towers.*
*These signs of daily life are good,*
*Even when by contrast something divine*
*Has injured the soul.*

"I don't think of divine things as injurious," I said.

"I don't think of them as anything else," said Ilona.

"Ah, the rooftops of home," said Sergeant Kohler, a plump and ruddy turnip of a man. "I've heard that the French trenches are pigsties, and the British are even worse."

"Of course, we do have our rats, but unlike the vermin in the Tommies' trenches they have no taste for human toes," said Leutnant Afflerbach with a slanted smile. "The form of dysentery you get here is far milder than the version the British are contracting. And unlike English lice, ours are edible."

"Herr Kohler, I must ask you not to speak ill of the British, or at least not of the Quincunx Battalion of the Second Bedfordshire Fusiliers," said Pochhammer. "For it happens we have orders to destroy that unit at dawn, part of the Neuve Chapelle counterattack dreamed up earlier today by Crown Prince Rupprecht."

"You're planning to annihilate the Quincunx Battalion, but you won't allow anyone to speak ill of them?" said a bewildered Werner.

"Leutnant Slevoght, allow me to educate you concerning class distinctions on the Western Front," said Pochhammer. "Thanks to a pair of paintings with which you are excruciatingly familiar, three categories of soldier occupy the trenches on both sides of no-man's-land. First we have the avatars of Kriegslust, zealous fighters seduced by Caligari's magnum opus. Then there are those who, having absorbed Fräulein Wessels's epic, embrace Lebenslust, love of life. Finally there are the Wehmutsvolk, the nostalgia infected, conscripts who never saw either painting and simply want to go home."

Conrad asked, "And this battalion—?"

"To a man they're of the Lebenslust persuasion," said Pochhammer. "They'll have great difficulty hating the Tommies they're expected to butcher tomorrow. Naturally I hope the Second Bedfordshire Fusiliers belong to the Lebenslust camp, or at least the Wehmutsvolk, but German Intelligence has thus far failed to answer that question." The Hauptmann bowed his head deferentially before the surrogate mother of his pacifist troops. "Fräulein, I would have you know we practice the art of hospitality around here. Our trench is your trench. Tonight you will sleep on my cot. Your companions, meanwhile, will enjoy the largesse of Korporal Jedermann, Sergeant Kohler, and Leutnant Afflerbach. You are welcome to observe tomorrow's engagement, as are Mr. Wyndham and Herr Röhrig, but until we ascertain the Weltanschauung of the enemy you should probably watch from the safety of this redoubt."

"Inarguably sage advice," I said.

"As for you, Leutnant," said Pochhammer to Werner, "perhaps you would like to second yourself to our battalion and participate in the engagement?"

"I no longer practice patriotism. It's bad for my health."

" 'The fruits are ripe, dipped in fire, cooked and sampled on earth,' " said Pochhammer. "I wish you all a good night's sleep."

Friday the 12th of March, day three of the Battle of Neuve Chapelle, began with the usual horrific cadence of the

Western Front. Salvo after salvo of artillery shells roared from the maws of howitzers and long-range cannons, whistled through the soft air of dawn, and exploded on contact with either the earth of no-man's-land (thereby eliminating barbed-wire entanglements) or a mud-and-sandbag barricade against which enemy soldiers were huddled (thereby eliminating undesirable human beings). Just then I couldn't tell which side had launched the barrage and which was enduring it, but I felt grateful that the bombs were bursting elsewhere than the 4th Battalion's trench.

I abandoned my mattress and by the light of the ascendant sun surveyed the sodden groove in which I'd spent the night. Werner and Conrad were sitting up in their cots, drinking coffee and exhibiting no ambition to rise, exit the trench, and observe current geopolitical events in no-man's-land. Like butterflies emerging from their chrysalises, Sergeant Kohler and Leutnant Afflerbach lay partially enveloped in two tattered sleeping bags, playing piquet. They did not remotely suggest soldiers about to participate in the great Neuve Chapelle counterattack, and neither did the rest of the battalion. Ilona was nowhere to be seen. Hauptmann Pochhammer and Korporal Jedermann were also gone, perhaps doing reconnaissance prior to the coming engagement.

I sought out the nearest ladder, then scurried to the topmost rung. Field glasses pressed against his gaze, Pochhammer crouched near the edge of the trench, flanked by Hans and—my heart sank—Ilona.

"Darling, please return to safety," I told her.

"*Guten Morgen*, young Francis. Something remarkable is about to occur."

A dense layer of restless fog blanketed no-man's-land, its wisps fingering the tree stumps and equine carcasses, its tendrils weaving amid the ungodly spirals of wire. The sound of tramping boots reached my ears, the footfalls of approaching soldiers, accompanied by the ratta-tat-tat of a snare drum. Suddenly a Quincunx Battalion flag (patterned to evoke the five dimples on a die) appeared above the fog bank, cutting through the sea of vapor like the dorsal fin of a shark, and then a second spotted flag emerged, then a third.

"They're marching out to meet us," noted Pochhammer.

"So their commander ordered a preemptive assault?" I asked.

"Not an assault exactly, but you could call it preemptive."

"How did they learn of Prince Rupprecht's intentions? Did a spy tell them?"

"This morning I disclosed my orders to Major Kemp on the far side of no-man's-land," said Pochhammer.

"You showed your orders to the enemy?"

"Not in person. Korporal Jedermann volunteered for the mission."

"As you might imagine, Kemp was grateful to learn of a potential threat to the Bedfordshire Fusiliers," said Hans. "The Tommies gave me tea and a Cadbury bar. They said I looked just like my portrait in Kleinbrück. I hadn't the heart to tell them the painting was burned."

"Pardon me, but do you chaps happen to know where they put the German Fourth?" cried a voice from deep within the fog bank (I couldn't say to which region of Britain his accent attested). "This bloody pea-souper has put us a bit off course!"

"You're in the right place!" Pochhammer shouted back.

"Jolly good! Lebenslust?"

"Lebenslust!" Pochhammer replied.

"Private Jenkins, Second Bedfordshire Fusiliers, Quincunx Battalion," said our visitor, emerging into visibility. He was a wide-eyed Tommy smartly equipped with new boots, a steel helmet, and a shiny bayonet.

"You are addressing Hauptmann Pochhammer of the Fafnirdrachen Riflemen. Perhaps you would care to salute me."

Private Jenkins did as Pochhammer suggested, then pivoted toward Hans. "Korporal, sir, might I have the privilege of giving you another piece of chocolate?"

"But of course," said Hans, approaching the awestruck Tommy.

As Private Jenkins bestowed a Cadbury bar on Ilona's creation, a second Tommy materialized, a snare drum riding on his thigh. After identifying himself as Private Bartlett, he gestured toward Ilona with fluttering fingers.

"Nigel, do you know who I think this is?" said Bartlett to Jenkins. "I think it's the artist lady!"

"Fräulein Wessels at your service," said Ilona.

"No, miss, we're at *your* service," said Bartlett.

Now a third Tommy appeared, presenting himself as Private Mallory.

"Alfie, you'll never guess," said Private Jenkins. "It's the lady who painted Korporal Jedermann."

"Blimey," gasped Private Mallory. He really said that.

By now the sun had burned away large sections of the fog bank, revealing hundreds of Tommies and a score of corporals and sergeants.

"And who might you be?" Private Jenkins asked me.

"Fräulein Wessels's art therapist."

"Therapist?" said Private Jenkins. "Why would she need a therapist?"

"When not tampering with history, I'm the Spider Queen of Ogygia," said Ilona.

Pochhammer made an about-face and barked an order into the trench. "Herr Kohler! Herr Afflerbach! Have the men fall in!"

In a matter of minutes all six hundred and eighty Fafnirdrachen Riflemen scrambled free of their muddy quarters, weapons in hand, spiked leather Pickelhauben on their heads. Thanks to the efforts of Sergeant Kohler and two dozen privates, four barrels of German beer (complete with spigots) went over the top along with the battalion, as did tin cups, sauce pans, shaving basins, and empty soup cans.

"Lebenslust!" the German soldiers cried in a single voice,

rushing pell-mell toward the British battalion.

"Lebenslust!" the Tommies chorused back.

*"Vita brevis, ars longa!"* cried Werner, emerging from the bastion.

Now Conrad climbed to the surface, offering his translation of Werner's Latin phrases—"Life is short, but art is eternal"—a saying I recognized as a garbled version (felicitously so, in my opinion) of a thought by Hippocrates.

The next thing I knew, the two battalions had intermingled like fingers fused in prayer, an inspiring alignment of bodies and Weltanschauungs, soldier encountering soldier with the incandescent ardor of lovers too long deprived of one another. Embraces were solicited and passionately accepted. Weapons were discarded willy-nilly, the resulting metallic tableau rescued from Dickensian sentimentality by the manifestly savage agenda of a bayonet, grenade, flamethrower, or infantry rifle. Kisses flew everywhere like coins flung into Eros's private pool, landing on cheeks, brows, necks, and, occasionally, lips.

For the better part of an hour, a kind of village fair unfolded on the field of the battle that hadn't happened. One could easily imagine Lorenzo the Hypnotist and Giacomo the Somnambulist pitching their tent in the vicinity. The soldiers exchanged cigarettes, toffee, and naughty French postcards. They learned each other's songs and ribald limericks. Fafnirdrachen Riflemen toasted Second Bedfordshire Fusiliers, and vice versa, with frothy measures of warm beer.

On orders from Sergeant Kohler, a platoon from the 4th Battalion climbed back into the trench and began dedicating the ladders and pallets to a new purpose. In less than an hour a network of makeshift footbridges spanned the German fortification, so that the beneficiaries of the improvised armistice could easily get from no-man's-land to occupied northern France.

"Defenders of Deutschland!" cried Pochhammer as he and Sergeant Kohler placed an empty beer barrel upright beside the widest bridge. "Guardians of Britain! A parting of the ways is upon us!" He climbed atop the barrel. "As a German Hauptmann and faithful soldier of Kaiser Wilhelm, I must stay here with Leutnant Afflerbach and the other commissioned officers! To the rest of you I say, '*Viel Glück*,' as you go forth to God knows where!"

"The Schwarzwald beckons!" yelled Sergeant Kohler.

"To the Schwarzwald!" chorused the entire German battalion.

"The Black Forest!" declared Private Jenkins.

"The Black Forest!" shouted the British battalion.

The Lebenslust troops collected their scattered guns (the better to hunt, poach, and persuade civilians to feed them) and assembled before the bridges. Not long after the soldiers began crossing over, the raw exhilaration of the moment possessed them, and they raised their voices in song.

*It's a long way to Tipperary,*

*It's a long way to go.*
*It's a long way to Tipperary*
*To the sweetest girl I know!*

"You're not going with them?" Ilona asked Hans.

"And leave my creator's side? Never."

"Your devotion is touching," said Ilona.

"Touching—but also transient," said Hans. "A Farbenmensch's time on this plane of existence is ephemeral."

*Goodbye, Piccadilly,*
*Farewell, Leicester Square!*
*It's a long, long way to Tipperary,*
*But my heart's right there.*

Conrad said, "And beyond this plane of existence lies . . . ?"

"I have no idea," said Hans, "but I keep thinking of Herr Slevoght's saying. How does it go? *Ars brevis . . .* ?"

"*Vita brevis, ars longa*," said Werner. "Life is short, but art is eternal."

"Yes, that's it. I have no idea what eternity is, dear friends, but I'll know the place when I get there."

# FIVE

I was hardly surprised when a shroud of melancholia descended on Hauptmann Pochhammer. While the rest of us enjoyed a fine lunch of pickled herring and hard cheese, he sat on his cot, drinking brandy from a flask and brooding about the abrupt disappearance of his purpose on earth. Gratified though he was that Lebenslust had triumphed over Kriegslust throughout his sector of the German line, he had no idea what to do next.

"As a fellow officer, give me your opinion, Leutnant Slevoght," said Pochhammer to Werner. "Shall I go to General Falkenhayn and tell him to court-martial me as an accessory to the mutiny that ended my command?"

"I see no point in that," said Werner. "I would rather you collaborated with us in destroying *Ecstatic Wisdom*."

"A laudable ambition," said Pochhammer.

"The flamethrower oil should work as the *coup de grâce*," said Werner, "but first we need . . . how does it go, Herr Hauptmann?"

"Some nonmilitary way to nullify Caligari's mercenaries," said Pochhammer, "lest we compromise Weizenstaat's neutrality and violate the Hague Conventions."

True, I was a mere painting master, not a military strategist. I understood the art of pictorial representation but not the art of war. And yet, gradually, inexorably, a possible method for murdering Caligari's magnum opus coalesced in my imagination.

"Hans, can you tell me more about that secret motorized pillbox in the Bois du Biez?" I asked Korporal Jedermann.

"I only know it was the main reason for the British attack on Neuve Chapelle."

"Ah, yes, the Landschiff," said Pochhammer. "The crazy vehicle actually exists—a prototype, that is, unless it was blown to pieces in the fighting. I know about the thing because a second cousin on my mother's side, Major Albrecht Mueller, was recently transferred to the Ministerium für Experimentelle Waffen as a combat-conditions weapons tester."

"Might I infer your cousin is in Neuve Chapelle right now?" I asked.

"Awaiting orders to drive the Landschiff into battle," said Pochhammer, nodding. "Unless a British bullet got him."

"That could work to our advantage," I said. "His proximity, I mean, not the bullet. Listen to my idea, everyone. Landschiff, meaning landship—right?—though in this case we're taking about a land-*battleship*: exactly the sort of vehicle that might accidently crash into a neutral country's art museum without violating the Hague Conventions, correct?"

"I'm no international lawyer," said Werner, "but that sounds right to me."

"Very clever, young Francis," said Ilona.

"*Ja*, except Albrecht and I aren't on speaking terms," said Pochhammer. "The blood we share is not thick—the same great-grandfather, a Prussian field marshal who fought Napoleon. To put it bluntly, we despise each other."

"Because he outranks you?" I asked.

"No."

"Politics? Religion?"

"Romance," said Pochhammer. "We're in love with the same woman."

"In France that would make you the best of friends," I said.

Pochhammer slid a tiny picture frame from his coat. "Would you like to see my true love's photograph? Dagmar Eschbach of Heidelberg. She is very beautiful. Last month Albrecht and I nearly resorted to pistols at dawn."

He passed the little portrait to me. Fräulein Eschbach was indeed beautiful, with extravagant blonde hair and ripe cheeks, though she also looked like a woman who enjoyed having men fight duels over her.

"Does Dagmar herself have an opinion in the matter?" asked Ilona.

"She loves us both equally and plans to marry a wealthy industrialist from Cologne named Horst."

"And how do you feel about the situation?" asked Ilona.

"It breaks my heart," said Pochhammer.

"Scoundrels are always named Horst," said Werner.

"Forgive my presumption, mein Herr," said Conrad to Pochhammer, "but I think I can end your pain and reconcile you with your cousin—a simple matter of freeing you from this fruitless preoccupation with Dagmar. Years ago Caligari and I were itinerant actors performing at village fairs. In the course of perfecting our show, we learned a great deal about the theory and practice of hypnotism."

"I can personally attest to Herr Röhrig's skill," said Ilona.

"I should explain that the method does not work in all cases," said Conrad, facing Pochhammer. "Only the most noble and rarefied souls are susceptible."

"*Merde de taureau.*"

"What?" said Werner.

"My mother speaks French," said Pochhammer.

"Please do this, mein Herr," said Ilona.

Flask in hand, Pochhammer rose from his cot and paced back and forth in the trench, absently soiling his boots with mud while lubricating his meditations with brandy.

"Very well," he said at last, "for the sake of Lebenslust, I shall submit to your technique. But after the war, Herr Röhrig, you and I must meet in my favorite Munich beer garden, and then, if I so request, you will give my pain back to me."

Thus it happened that on the 13th of March, 1915, shortly after noon, the Battle of Neuve Chapelle having ended in the usual Western Front stalemate, six would-be saboteurs set off northward from Loos along the German line, a party that included a congenial Korporal from an inaccessible dimension and a recently hypnotized Hauptmann no longer in love with a beauty named Dagmar. Werner and I took turns carrying the flamethrower. Every so often a Schütze on sentry duty would appear in our path, straightaway summoning a superior officer, but in every case Pochhammer convinced the officer that we should be allowed to pursue our mission of "bringing to General Falkenhayn this experimental Flammenwerfer, capable of destroying an entire platoon in a single blast."

Shortly before dusk we reached Neuve Chapelle, recently reoccupied by units from Kaiser Wilhelm's Third Army. Evidence of the artillery barrages was everywhere on view: black craters, charred timbers, scattered bricks, walls that now resembled cross-sections of mountain ranges. We proceeded to the solitary inn, La Pucelle d'Orléans. Despite our muddy clothes and disheveled demeanors, the morose and elderly landlord, M. Laux, phlegmatically provided Hauptmann Pochhammer with a key to the one remaining room (our host's mood was doubtless soured by our leader's German uniform). Questioned by Pochhammer, M. Laux disclosed that a dozen officers from Falkenhayn's VII Corps were living at the inn, including a Major Albrecht

Mueller—though Mueller had made it clear that no one, whether German, Austrian, or Etente, should be told the location of his room.

Pochhammer commandeered from M. Laux a sheet of paper and a stubby wooden pencil. He composed a message, then instructed the landlord's grandson (a skinny, gap-toothed waif) to deliver it posthaste.

> *Dear Cousin Albrecht,*
>
> *For reasons that elude me, my heart no longer belongs to Dagmar. From this moment on, your courtship of her will proceed with my blessing. I may even join with you in trying to discourage the odious Horst.*
>
> *Owing to the vicissitudes of war, I am presently in Neuve Chapelle, staying at this very inn. It is imperative that my associates and I meet with you, at a time and place of your choosing, to discuss a strategic necessity involving the Landschiff.*
>
> *Sincerely,*
> *Günter Pochhammer*
> *Hauptmann, Deutsches Heer*

Not surprisingly, Major Mueller's return communiqué accused his correspondent of being an imposter looking to steal information about the experimental weapon for the Entente. In his next message Pochhammer cleverly allayed that suspicion by enclosing his photograph of Dagmar (on the back of which he'd written, "All's fair in love and war, but I give her to you anyway"). Mueller responded with a note proposing a 10:00 a.m. meeting by the fountain in the village square.

Over the next two hours we bestowed on ourselves, serially and sybaritically, the pleasures of a warm bath, languidly soaking the Western Front out of our flesh—the mud, the lice, the stench, the rat dropings. By unanimous agreement Ilona received the bed, while the remainder of our party, after hunting up stray blankets throughout the inn, collapsed on the floor in improvised sleeping bags.

"Young Francis, I am having a revolution," said Ilona.

"A revelation."

"Herr Hauptmann, I would like to borrow the second note from your cousin, also the landlord's pencil," Ilona told Pochhammer. He obliged her without comment. She promptly drew a numeral 8 on the back of the sheet, then displayed it to her fellow saboteurs. "Meine Herren, what does this number mean to you?"

"Eight planets," said Pochhammer.

"Eight arms on an octopus," said Conrad.

"Eight pawns to a rank," said Werner.

"Seven dwarves plus a princess," said Hans.

"Naturally I think of you," I told Ilona. "I think of my four-eyed, eight-legged Spider Queen of Ogygia."

"Exactly—now watch what happens when I rotate the page ninety degrees," she said, turning her drawing. "What do we get?"

"A fallen eight," said Hans.

"A *pince-nez*," said Conrad.

"We get the symbol for infinity," said Ilona. "We get the emblem of my father."

"Most ingenious," I said. "And to you this suggests. . . ?"

"That I did not hate him after all," she said. "That he had good reasons for being himself. That I loved him as much as I love my spiders."

"*Bien joué*, Ilona," I said evenly.

"A great burden has been lifted from me," said Ilona. "Arachnophilia. Filial affection. It's all the same."

"Indubitably," I said, though not fully convinced.

"Sleep is also therapeutic," noted Pochhammer.

"I can tell you with some confidence that Freud would greatly appreciate your self-analysis," Werner said to Ilona, "and Caligari would detest it."

"And I intend to share my discovery with neither gentleman," said Ilona.

The following morning, after coffee and rolls at the inn, we betook ourselves to the village fountain, a baroque marble sculpture that had somehow survived the shelling. Major Mueller awaited us beside a pair of sculpted dolphins spewing water from their mouths. A well-favored man with spectacles and a neatly trimmed moustache, he was taller, rangier, and more hirsute than his second cousin. For a full minute the two young officers silently inspected each other, then shook hands, then embraced.

"It is most gallant of you to cede Dagmar to me," said Mueller.

"Gallant with only a soupçon of resentment," said Pochhammer. "And now you will kindly show us the Landschiff."

"It's a beautiful machine."

"Take us to it."

"That is quite impossible."

"Herr Major, I present to you Leutnant Slevoght, veteran of the Marne; Mr. Wyndham, painting master at Träumenchen Asylum; Korporal Jedermann, a conscript in a phantom army; and Fräulein Wessels, a sorceress from Kleinbrück."

"On the day I left the nursery, I stopped believing in ghosts and witches," said Mueller. "I suggest we take this conversation in a different direction."

"Herr Hauptmann, I must once again ask for your cousin's second note and the landlord's pencil," said Ilona. "Also your Hölderlin."

Pochhammer complied. Using the poetry volume as a drawing board, Ilona sketched a hasty but uncannily accurate portrait of Major Mueller, cleverly incorporating the infinity sign by turning it into his spectacles. She fixed intently on her creation.

A full minute elapsed—a second minute—and then the cranium of the illustrated Major flipped back like the lid of a waffle iron, revealing his naked brain. A bright yellow canary popped out of the right hemisphere, flew to the edge of the sheet, and disappeared.

"A conjurer's illusion," said Mueller with forced nonchalance. Sweat trickled down his temples. "Though extremely persuasive."

"Cousin Albrecht," said Pochhammer, "you must believe me when I say that the quantity of immoral magic corrupting this war is far greater than the generals will admit."

From the figure's left cerebral hemisphere a rainbow emerged, opening like a coquette's fan. The multicolored arch transmuted into a moth and fluttered away.

"Tell me, Herr Major, are some of the soldiers under your command unusually fond of carnage?" asked Pochhammer. "Are they insane with Kriegslust?"

"True enough. Can you shed some light on this mystery?"

"An imbalanced mystic named Caligari did it to them. By a series of uncanny coincidences, we are well situated to sabotage his project with the help of your beautiful machine."

"Please don't tell us that, after marching all the way

from Loos to Neuve Chapelle, we're not even allowed to *see* the Landschiff," I said.

Mueller frowned and clucked his tongue. "Follow me."

Throughout our twenty-minute hike to the Bois du Biez, Werner supplied the Major with a terse narrative of the present crisis: the infantry columns parading past *Ecstatic Wisdom*, Ilona's heroic but short-lived antidote, our plan to incinerate the beast with ensorcelled oil, the political impossibility of a frank military assault. Although Mueller confessed that he found Werner's story "less credible than the ravings of a shell-shock victim," he nevertheless noted, "I am intrigued by the logistical challenges it poses," and as we approached the Landschiff's hiding place—a large windowless shed surrounded by oaks and elms—he announced that as his opening move he would arrange for General Dressler at the Ministerium für Experimentelle Waffen to receive "a disingenuous letter from his most experienced weapons tester—that is, myself."

"You would lie to a superior officer?" said Pochhammer.

"I've had lots of practice," said Mueller. "You must understand that Dressler and the whole M.E.W. hate any experimental weapon that doesn't have wings. They believe this war and all future wars will be decided by Fliegende Festungen, flying fortresses. Dressler will be delighted to learn that the Landschiff has been so radically reimagined here in Neuve Chapelle that its civilian designers in Berlin recently reclassified it as an aeroplane."

"I thought it was a battleship on caterpillar treads," I said.

"Indeed," said Mueller.

"So it *hasn't* been reclassified?"

"Of course not. In his exhilaration over the weapon's new identity, General Dressler will grant my request to fly the prototype four hundred kilometers to the southeast so I can test it during the imminent German attack on Verdun."

"Is a German attack on Verdun imminent?" asked Pochhammer.

"It's probably a year away, but Dressler will pretend he knows it's about to happen, lest he lose face with his weapons tester."

"Won't the designers in Berlin be angry at you for putting words in their mouths?" I asked.

"They won't know about my letter. Since when do civilian engineers and technologically illiterate generals talk to each other? This cabal of ours needs a leader, dear Günter."

"You outrank the rest of us, dear Albrecht," said Pochhammer.

Mueller swung back the shed door, admitting an eddy of dead leaves and a piercing shaft of sunlight. Slowly and solemnly, as if it entering the nave of a cathedral, we crossed the threshold. The gritty stink of petroleum pervaded the air. Bristling with rivets, plated with armor, an immense rhomboidal vehicle loomed out of the shadows like a lozenge devised to soothe Gargantua's sore throat. The Landschiff's most forbidding aspects were the fixed turrets bulging from her hull, two little castles equipped with three-inch guns, but her *sine qua non* was obviously the pair of segmented conveyor belts encircling her flanks like oval picture frames.

Greasy engine parts lay scattered across the floor. Mechanics in stained overalls scurried about the shed gripping welding torches and adjustable wrenches. Suddenly a hatch atop the hull popped open, and a stringy little man in an oil-stained uniform emerged holding a screwdriver the size of a gladius. He offered Mueller a grandiloquent salute. The Major reciprocated succinctly, then introduced the noncommissioned officer as "Sergeant Görlitz, chief mechanic on the Landschiff crew" and presented us as an inspection committee from Nuremburg who wanted to know "if the weapon would stay in one piece during a test run from here to Kleinbrück."

"To Kleinbrück?" said Görlitz. "No, Herr Major. Right now it would fall apart during a test run from here to the privy."

"We're taking it to Kleinbrück anyway—on a secret mission I can't discuss with you," said Mueller.

"But Kleinbrück is in a neutral country."

"Let me worry about that. Sergeant, I bring peculiar news. The engineers in Berlin have reclassified our Landschiff as an aeroplane."

"As a what?"

"Aeroplane."

"How ambitious of them. Will they be reclassifying our

U-boats as field artillery?"

"It's a bizarre decision, I know," said Mueller.

"Entirely bizarre, Herr Major. Of course, if the engineers in Berlin wish to reclassify me as a war hero living in Tahiti on a generous pension, I would not object."

Although the Ministerium für Experimentelle Waffen took its own sweet time pondering Major Mueller's letter, they reacted exactly as he'd predicted. General Dressler wrote that he was "extremely pleased" by the reclassification of the Landschiff, and he declared that Mueller was "hereby ordered to test the prototype during the imminent Verdun offensive." The final paragraph of Dressler's reply was particularly gratifying.

> *Should you be forced to make an emergency landing between Neuve Chapelle and the fortresses on the Meuse, this letter will serve to alert French and Belgian citizens in the German-occupied areas of Champagne and the Ardennes that they must cooperate with you or risk reprisals. In closing, let me commend your on-site mechanics for recognizing that the new weapon should have been an aeroplane all along.*

Although Mueller had appointed himself our leader, it was Werner who now proceeded to impose a strict calendar on our mission. His reasoning was impeccable. The attack on the painting must occur on April the 4th, Easter Sunday, when Caligari would surely have suspended the usual procession, inadvertently enabling us to crash the Landschiff into the museum without the complication of new recruits arriving on the scene from Kleinbrück Station.

As if to reassert his authority, Major Mueller made two tactical decisions of manifest brilliance. He ordered the three-inch guns removed from the turrets, "thus demonstrating our respect for Weizenstaat's neutrality," and he divided our party into two groups, "for it's essential we send Leutnant Slevoght, Herr Röhrig, Fräulein Wessels, and Korporal Jedermann—Task Force One—ahead to Kleinbrück to reconnoiter the target." The four would travel by motorcar along with the delicate and invaluable flamethrower, Mueller having requisitioned a Mercedes upon being seconded to the M.E.W. As for our eventual rendezvous, the Major suggested that we gather at the main hostelry (probably the only hostelry) in the Luxembourg village of Gheldaele near the Weizenstaat border, no later than 11:00 p.m. on April the 3rd, "a good seven hours before the sun rises on our Savior's empty tomb."

At ten o'clock on the morning of March 31st, 1915, her fuel tank filled with petrol, her turrets stripped of their guns, and her cab crammed with Task Force Two, the Landschiff rolled out of the Bois du Biez and began traveling south through occupied France. Mueller and Pochhammer took turns steering the beast—a matter of watching the oncoming road through a forward window and swerving left or right by making one caterpillar tread spin faster than the other. Although our company comprised only Sergeant Görlitz, the cousins, and myself (the others having set off in the Mercedes two days earlier), the space was absurdly congested, and I found myself wishing the vehicle would break down just so I could escape my sardine circumstances and breathe some fresh air.

We moved at a good fifteen kilometers per hour, getting all the way to Cambrai by late afternoon (despite a woefully flawed map). So formidable in appearance was our terrestrial battleship that every category of passerby—German reservists on the march, *bergeres* herding their flocks, *bonnes femmes* going to market, children riding their bicycles to school—accorded us a wide berth. The Landschiff owned the roads. The rattled citizens of Cambrai readily surrendered their petrol stores (no need to intimidate them with General Dressler's letter). We filled the fuel tank and resumed our journey, reaching Le Cateau by nightfall. Although our vehicle boasted battery-powered headlamps, they kept conking out, and so instead of pressing on we bivouacked in a cow pasture.

Day two brought a festival of disasters. Shortly before ten o'clock the left tread snapped, and Mueller and Görlitz spent two hours splicing it together with bolts and barbed wire.

At one o'clock the right tread came apart, another delay, another improvised repair. As twilight stole over the outskirts of Guise, the vehicle began hemorrhaging oil, and it took Görlitz so long to replace the blown gasket that we could go no farther that evening.

Against my expectations, the following day elapsed without a single catastrophe. On reaching Guise we turned abruptly east, then traveled halfway to Sedan on the Meuse before losing the light.

Day four proved equally felicitous, Pochhammer piloting us efficiently along a network of logging roads through the Belgian Ardennes, then across Luxembourg to within a kilometer of the border village of Gheldaele. I glanced at my pocket watch. Seven forty-five p.m. We had beaten the eleven o'clock deadline with over three hours to spare.

Upon assuming the controls, Major Mueller steered the Landschiff into a sheltering grove of maples and braked it to a full stop. He shut off the engine. Leaving Görlitz in charge, the Major led Pochhammer and myself into the village, where we soon spotted the Mercedes parked in front of a hostelry called Der Bettler zu Pferd—the Beggar on Horseback.

Whistling insouciantly, sabotage being the last thing on our minds (oh, yes), we entered the cramped and shabby dining room. Werner, Conrad, Hans, and Ilona sat at a booth, contemplating blue ceramic steins. My beloved looked ravishing in her gabardine trench coat and cloche hat. We embraced and kissed.

"We've secured lodgings for everyone," said Ilona.

"The first step in defeating immoral magic is to get a good night's sleep," noted Werner.

The cousins took hold of an unoccupied table and appended it to the booth. Mueller ordered a round for our entire party. The tankards arrived promptly, crested with Bavarian spindrift.

"In recent days Conrad has proven adept at espionage," said Ilona.

"I have become a creature of the shadows, slinking around without Caligari's knowledge," said Conrad. "All the signs bode well for tomorrow's raid. Herr Direktor has decided to give most of his janissaries an Easter vacation. Only two will be on duty, stationed on the steps outside the museum. A regular Träumenchen sentry will guard the interior passageway to the gallery."

From his shirt pocket Werner retrieved a sheet of paper, spreading it open on the table. Rendered with Cubist élan, the drawing offered an overhead view of the museum.

"While Task Force Two was enjoying a motor tour through northern France, the rest of us collaborated on a scenario," said Werner.

"I'm still our leader, Leutnant," noted Mueller.

"Of course, Herr Major," said Werner. "Here's what's going to happen. Tomorrow morning I'll drive Conrad and

Hauptmann Pochhammer over the Moselle River to Kleinbrück. We'll leave the Mercedes in the village, then cross the footbridge. Conrad will enter the asylum through the main gate, slip into the château, and approach the sentry guarding the gallery."

"Herr Jerabek has always detested Caligari," noted Conrad. "I'll convince him he has nothing to gain by trying to prevent Herr Direktor's overthrow. If necessary, Jerabek and I will raise the elevator platform."

"At precisely seven o'clock, zero hour, Hauptmann Pochhammer and I will unholster our Mausers and surprise the janissaries on the steps outside the museum," said Werner. "We'll order them to throw down their arms—and then we'll point to the runaway Landschiff and suggest they flee. A few minutes later, Major Mueller will crash his vehicle into the south wall of the museum, knocking it down and—"

"And destroying my spiders," said Ilona drily. "Also Gaston's chess pieces."

"It can't be helped," said Werner. "Next Major Mueller will drive across the elevator platform and ram *Ecstatic Wisdom* head on, so the entire west wall collapses and the traumatized painting lands face up on the ruins. An instant later somebody will rush onto the scene with the flamethrower—"

"I could be that person," said Ilona.

"I won't allow it," I said.

"Fräulein, it's out of the question," said Werner.

"It's *absolutely* out of the question, O my creator," said Hans. "I would volunteer, but as a Farbenmensch I might be torn from this plane at any moment."

Werner continued, "Somebody will rush onto the scene—"

"Sergeant Görlitz loves daredevil missions," said Mueller.

"Sergeant Görlitz will rush onto the scene—"

"No, *I* want to do it," I blurted out, my words running recklessly ahead of my rational faculties. The sleep of reason breeds martyrs. "I *must* do it. Seven months ago Caligari's magic almost burned me alive."

"Young Francis, you've never operated a flamethrower," protested Ilona.

"It's easier to use than a flush toilet," said Pochhammer.

"Mr. Wyndham will rush onto the scene and incinerate the painting," said Werner, "and then we'll all escape in the Landschiff and the motorcar."

"This is a good plan," said Mueller.

Throughout the remainder of the evening much beer was consumed and few words were exchanged. Saboteurs are a quiet fellowship. Shortly after midnight Mueller announced that he intended to sleep in the vehicle, guarding it along with Görlitz. I followed him into an April night as sticky as gesso.

We proceeded to the Mercedes and obtained the flamethrower. Mueller showed me how to install an igniter in the nozzle—naturally Task Force One hadn't traveled all the way to Luxembourg with an armed flamethrower bouncing around in the trunk—and light the wick with an ordinary wooden match. For our dress rehearsal we hiked a full kilometer into a soggy, fallow field studded with brown stalks. An unemployed scarecrow rose before us. I aimed the nozzle and vaporized the effigy in a single blast. Briefly the stalks became a morass of flames, sparks, and smoke, but then the blaze died, smothered by the damp earth.

"Whatever happens tomorrow, don't release the lever, or you'll have to stop and insert a fresh igniter," said Mueller, taking the flamethrower in hand. "Keep on firing. Never let the enemy regroup."

"You'd rather see Sergeant Görlitz fight the painting, wouldn't you?" I said, surveying the scarecrow's charred remains. "You don't think I can do the job."

"It's after midnight," said the Major, glancing at his pocket watch. "Happy Easter, Mr. Wyndham. You're going to be sensational, fantastic, *wunderbar*. And when the battle's won, we'll decorate a bunch of eggs and stick them up Dr. Caligari's ass."

While cocks cried the astonishing news called dawn, and milk cows lowed their sisters awake, Ilona and I stood outside Der Bettler zu Pferd and watched as the Mercedes left Gheldaele, bound for Kleinbrück. We took each other's hands and walked to the maple grove through the sacrosanct air of Easter morning. Naturally I wished Ilona had been willing to stay in the hostelry with Hans, but she wouldn't hear of it. "This time around," she told me, "I must be by your side when you enter the arena."

I scurried up the stern ladder to the roof of the Landschiff and rapped on the hatch. Sergeant Görlitz appeared, chomping on an apple, and admitted us.

"We weren't expecting the witch," said Mueller.

"Fuck you," said Ilona.

The Major started the engine, put it in gear, and backed the vehicle out of the grove. Ten minutes later, we lumbered without incident past a sign reading WILLKOMMEN IN WEIZENSTAAT. On reaching the outskirts of Kleinbrück, Mueller pivoted north and followed the west bank of the Moselle toward the museum. He brought us to within thirty meters of the south wall, then applied the brakes and set the engine to idling.

Six-forty a.m. Twenty minutes to zero hour. I opened the hatch, then lifted the flamethrower, armed with a fresh igniter, through the aperture and laid it on the roof. As I climbed out of the hot cab, a soft rain moistened my brow and cheeks. I welcomed the cool droplets. They did not portend a storm, and even if they did, what storm could be ferocious enough to extinguish the fire I meant to hurl against *Ecstatic Wisdom*?

Ilona appeared on the roof bearing a carpetbag filled

with spare igniters. I scrambled down the stern ladder. She lowered the flamethrower into my grasp, then descended.

Abruptly a human figure appeared beside the Landschiff, our dear Korporal Jedermann, breathless and sweating, his rifle strapped to his shoulder. Apparently he'd run all the way from the hostelry.

"O my creator," he said.

I understood immediately why he'd come. My throat constricted. Sorrow flooded my flesh.

"I can't be with you anymore." Hans's tears mingled with the raindrops on his face. "A Farbenmensch is not a *mensch* at all. What a wretched advertisement I am for eternity."

"My poor child," said Ilona, kissing the Korporal's cheek.

"Goodbye, Piccadilly," he said.

"Farewell, Leicester Square," she said.

"We love you," I said.

"You are truly a *mensch*," she said.

Hans became filmy and blurred. Gradually, brushstroke by magical brushstroke, particle by mystic particle, he lost his purchase on the world, devolving toward the status of an unpainted oil, an unwritten poem, an uncarved statue, an unwoven tapestry.

"It's a long, long way to Tipperary," he said, melding with the morning air.

"But my heart's right there," said Ilona.

"Your greatest work," I told her.

"Better than my spiderwebs, certainly. But don't all

artists believe their greatest work is still to come?"

Major Mueller put the Landschiff in gear. The treads began their screeching revolutions, and the vehicle moved grindingly forward. Ilona helped me shoulder the heavy cylinder, then lit the igniter wick with a wooden match from the carpetbag.

As the Landschiff approached the target, its velocity increased. Positioned behind the tailpipe, plagued by the black noxious fumes, I tried to sprint (as if I were still on the track team back at Boalsburg High), but the flamethrower held me to a trot. Despite grief, fear, nausea, and carbon monoxide, my progress was punctuated by bursts of exultation. For my previous attack on the painting I'd armed myself with a mere canister of turpentine. Today I had on my side a motorized pillbox, a benevolent sorceress, and a flamethrower filled with supernatural distillates.

With a ground-wrenching explosion, its thunder equal to any artillery shell that had ever burst on the Western Front, the Landschiff smashed through the south wall, doubtless ruining Ilona's oils and Gaston's watercolors. The vehicle continued on its way, leaving behind a gaping hole and, courtesy of the unfallen stones, a kind of Expressionist Roman arch. Rubble cascaded into my path, but I dodged each spinning chunk without losing my balance. The vehicle swerved to the left and, slipping between the vertical chains, crossed the elevator platform and continued moving. I charged into the breach, the blessed rain cooling my flesh, the cylinder gnawing my spine. Cautiously but quickly I climbed atop a mound of marble shards, then steeled myself for the second crash.

Caligari's nihilistic masterwork hung in its customary location. A sudden gust of wind tore the curtain away, exposing the painted surface of the canvas to the rain—or perhaps the picture, sensing our intentions, had deliberately shed its mantle. Now came the collision, the Landschiff slitting the canvas top to bottom and shattering the west wall. The stones, falling, carried *Ecstatic Wisdom* down with them. Mueller threw his machine into reverse, traveled backward over the platform, and stopped a meter short of the east wall. I descended from my hill and rushed toward the wounded picture. Firming my grip on the rubber hose, I positioned myself at the bottom edge of the stretcher frame, perpendicular to the canvas, and surveyed the beautiful marching recruits by the rain-veiled light of the Easter sun. They fixed me with their seductive stares. The voice of the nearest soldier filled my head.

*Come with us, my friend. Join our sacred brotherhood. Heed the call to arms. You need this battle. You desire it more than life itself.*

Naturally I would like to report that this exhortation did not affect me—and yet for the flicker of an instant I found myself in thrall to the painting's consecrated nonsense.

"Young Francis, wake up!" screamed Ilona.

I aimed the nozzle and depressed the lever.

*"Auf Wiedersehen!"* I told the soldier.

Nothing happened. Again I depressed the lever. No flame came forth. I checked the igniter. The wick was dormant. My kingdom for a match.

And suddenly Ilona was beside me, pulling a Streichhölzer box from her carpetbag. She lit a match. The rain extinguished it. She lit a second match, cupping it with her palm, and touched it to the wick. Within the igniter a glorious little flame flourished.

I aimed the nozzle and depressed the lever. The propellant gas performed admirably, sending a gush of eager, enchanted, flammable oil coursing toward the burning wick. The rubber hose vibrated in my hands. Torrents of fire spiraled forth as if from the nostrils of Fafnir himself. Raindrops evaporated as they hit the white-hot nozzle. The pigments ignited, the gesso went up in flames, and the stretcher bars supplied kindling to the conflagration.

Just then the museum doors flew back, admitting a mountainous janissary, black-bearded, furious, a pistol in his hand. Had this giant shot Werner? Gunned down Hauptmann Pochhammer? Had Werner or Pochhammer killed the other janissary? I'd heard no pistol reports, but the Landschiff's engine might have drowned them out.

Smoke rolled forth in billows so black and vast I could no longer see the painting. Sparks danced in the opaque cloud. My eyes, beset by ten thousand particulates, released streams of tears. I coughed convulsively. By summoning all my reserves of determination, I kept the lever depressed—never let the enemy regroup, Mueller had said—as I swept the nozzle back and forth, crisscrossing the canvas with rippling cords of flame.

Just beyond the top of the painting, the smoke abruptly parted to reveal the bearded janissary, his pistol arm rigid and outstretched, as if he were fighting a duel. He took aim at my head. He fired. Ilona screamed. The projectile drilled through my skull and traversed my brain, killing me, then presumably exited through the back wall of my cranium, littering the gallery floor with petals of bone, though by then the bullet's trajectory was for me a matter of complete indifference.

# SIX

I had never died before. While the living are well within their rights to rail against the many pathologies through which a person might become a corpse, oblivion itself is beyond evaluation. The lambent void enjoys no presence. The abyss is bereft of qualities. Mein Herr, Agent Thanatos has nothing to report.

And yet in my case death's requisite oblivion was curiously incomplete. For all the silence, pallor, and ethereality of my circumstances, I understood myself to be upright, spine straight, walking somewhere. In time I could perceive my surroundings: a fogbound bridge not unlike the setting of Edvard Munch's *The Scream*. Arrayed in mist, a human figure hobbled toward me.

"Mr. Wyndham?"

So I'd also retained my sense of hearing, faint but functional.

"Mr. Wyndham, is that you?"

It was Hans Jedermann, holding his rifle in one hand, waving at me with the other.

"Am I in fact dead?" I asked.

"Yes, but your Doppelgänger is not. At present you inhabit a simulacrum of yourself. Follow me."

For what seemed like an hour Hans and I walked side by side through the fog, saying nothing. I'd had no idea the *Scream* bridge was so long. Eventually we came to an empty stretcher frame, tall and narrow like a clothier's mirror.

"Cross over, Mr. Wyndham," said Hans. "Fräulein Wessels needs you."

"Will this take me to Kleinbrück?"

"Cross over."

So I held my breath, stepped through the aperture . . .

And stumbled into the nocturnal sitting room of my Träumenchen apartments. Haggard, drained, and doleful, Werner sat on the divan. The gas-lamps disclosed the usual art supplies strewn across the worktable: brushes, palette, knife, linseed oil, mustard pots filled with bewitched pigments. The casement window framed a gibbous moon and a scattering of stars.

"Let me be the first to congratulate you," said Werner. "You shut down Caligari's war machine. *Ecstatic Wisdom* is nothing but a pile of ashes. Well done, Francis."

"Evidently the victory cost me my life."

Bit by bit, my sensorium was restored to me. I caught a whiff of linseed oil. Werner's voice grew louder.

"Blame that disaster on me if you wish," he said. "The plan of attack was mostly my creation."

"Where's Ilona?"

Ignoring my question, Werner gestured toward the paint pots. "Conrad buried them under the sundial as she'd instructed him. I dug them up at her request. Their magic was obviously intact."

"I can't believe that I'm . . ."

"Alas, 'dead' is the correct word. Pochhammer and I easily intimidated the smaller janissary, but the other one broke away and ran into the ruined gallery. Not long after the giant put a bullet in your brain, Pochhammer shot him through the heart. Look behind you, Francis."

I turned and surveyed the stretcher frame, which from my present vantage displayed a taut canvas tacked to the bars. Poised on an easel, the painting confused me at first, but then I realized that, in leaving the uncanny bridge and entering the sitting room, I'd passed through a full-length portrait of myself. Ilona had captured my countenance in full: the mole on my jaw, the greenish tint of my irises, the little white scar above my lip—memento of a fall from a tree house. She'd dressed me in my customary blue flannel shirt and brown corduroy trousers. The paint was not yet dry.

"What time is it?"

"Eleven o'clock post meridiem," said Werner, consulting his pocket watch. "Technically you're one of those Easter resurrectees. As soon as Caligari saw the Landschiff, he started waving his pistol around and fulminating about the Hague Conventions. When Mueller informed him the machine was unarmed, Caligari kept on screaming, so the Major told him to go to hell, then drove off toward Luxembourg with Sergeant Görlitz. Shortly thereafter, Pochhammer left in the Mercedes."

"Where's Ilona?" I asked again.

"I understand your sense of urgency."

Werner led me out of my apartments, then down the corridor to the grand lobby. Inmates milled about, several in their delusional regalia—harlequin, highwayman, Queen Cleopatra. Upon entering the north wing, we strode past the troubadour tapestries to Conrad's quarters. Werner knocked on the door. Conrad appeared instantly, a lit cigarette dangling from his lower lip, a cracked china teacup in his hand. He looked me up and down.

"I never doubted she could bring you back." He took a drag, tapped the ashes into the teacup, then ushered me into his foyer and along a gloomy hallway. "She loved you very much."

As I entered Conrad's gas-lit back parlor, I was assailed by a cacophony of shrieks—my own, probably, but it sounded like a chorus. Could it be that Munch's figure on the bridge, hands pressed against his cheeks and ears, was not screaming at all but instead sought to block out the whole mad, howling universe? Like Ophelia's corpse floating down a river in Elsinore, Ilona lay on a velvet couch, arms folded across her breast. Her dead eyes were open. She wore her yellow blouse and gray Punjabi pants. Dropping to my knees, I kissed her cold lips, then took her hands in mine. I buried my face in her hair, which had never fully recovered from last year's scissors attack.

"The janissary shot her in the stomach," said Werner. "Then Pochhammer killed the janissary."

"We wanted to take her to the sanitarium surgeon, but she insisted on finishing your portrait," said Conrad. "She was in great pain. It was all entirely horrible and operatic."

"Ludwig, Pietro, and Gaston did the stretching and the priming," said Werner, "and at noon she began turning you into a Farbenmensch. Shortly after sunset she applied the last stroke . . . and then she died."

For a full hour I sat on the rug beside Ilona, rocking back and forth, sobbing, keening, rubbing the mucus from my nose with Conrad's handkerchief. My desolation engaged my whole body—ligaments, muscles, arteries, bones: I hadn't realized grief was such an exhausting business.

"Many months ago Ilona told me that one day she'd be compelled to paint my portrait."

"You don't quite understand what she accomplished," said Conrad. "Her interpretation of Francis Wyndham is more amazing than you realize."

He took me to a private gallery in the deepest reaches of his domain, then lit the lamps to disclose walls hung with full-color lithographed posters from the days he and

Caligari had toured the countryside. SEE GIACOMO THE SOMNAMBULIST SWALLOW A SWORD . . . EAT A TORCH . . . CATCH A BULLET IN HIS TEETH. The centerpiece of the exhibit was the upright cabinet in which Giacomo had supposely slept when not on exhibition, its dual lids meeting in a zigzag seam.

Conrad opened the cabinet. Stiff, naked, and vertical, a male corpse of medium build occupied the compartment. Someone had pulled a brown jute bag over the head, giving the cadaver the appearance of a hanged criminal.

"The janissary didn't know how the flamethrower worked, so after he shot you, he opened the cylinder and poured the rest of the oil on your head," said Conrad. "He applied a firebrand. Your face melted away from your skull. Then the janissary shot Ilona. Then Pochhammer put a bullet in his heart."

"So she painted me . . ."

"From memory."

"The late Francis Wyndham had considerable ability," I said, "but he could never have accomplished such a feat."

"Happily, his simulacrum needn't duplicate Ilona's achievement in every way," said Conrad.

"The students have been busy all day," said Werner. "The canvas is stretched and primed. The gesso is almost dry. When do you wish to begin?"

"Right after sunrise," I said. "The light will be perfect."

I felt no particular need to pray, fast, or shave my head. What mattered was to activate whatever supernatural gifts my beloved creator had bestowed on me. Under Werner's supervision, Ludwig, Pietro, and Gaston carried the closed cabinet into my sitting room. The space glowed with intimations of day. Ilona's portrait of me was now propped against the casement. My students set the cabinet beside a blank, vertical canvas clamped to the easel.

"I wish you hadn't destroyed my watercolors," said Gaston. "Or Fräulein Wessels's spiderweb oils, for that matter."

"In war there is always collateral damage," said Werner.

"We ask your forgiveness," I told the Grandmaster.

"Move twenty: White dispatches a rook to queen one, and then his game begins falling apart," said Gaston.

After the students had exited the room, Conrad rotated the jigsaw-puzzle doors to reveal a perpendicular, open-eyed Ilona, lashed to my own earthly remains, my head still obscured by the jute bag. Paralyzed with horror, I stared mutely at the macabre tableau, then told my friends I couldn't abide the thought of contemplating her corpse for a protracted interval. Conrad suggested a looking-glass. I gave my assent. Within the hour, through a clever deployment of alchemical fixtures from Caligari's atelier, Conrad succeeded in setting up a circular mirror adjacent to the easel, so that, when I positioned myself between the canvas and the cabinet, Ilona's face filled the glass.

"Today you will be the equal of Munch, Cézanne, and

Picasso," said Werner.

"And then you will astonish Paris with an apple," said Conrad.

My friends left me to my labors. With my graphite stick I drew her facial contours on the dried gesso, then sketched in the rest of her. I remembered how, on the afternoon when we'd first made love, she'd spoken of wanting a satin gown that matched her hair. And now an unexpected metaphysical opportunity had arisen.

Hour after hour, palette in one hand, brush in the other, I worked without stopping, conjuring her lovely face. I made a point of fully restoring her exuberant tresses, using vermilion mixed with a dash of cadmium yellow. For her Grecian-style gown I employed the exact same hue. I gave my love her guileless but knowing smile.

With the coming of dusk I transferred a daub of ultramarine from the palette to my smallest brush. I added an impossibly blue highlight to each iris, then stepped away from the canvas, weary but satisfied.

"I need you," I told the portrait. The image remained inert. "Come to me, my dearest." No specter rippled the canvas. "I love you so very much."

Doubtless Farbenmensch sorcery required patience of its practitioners. I closed the cabinet doors, so that the mirror, reflecting the zigzag seam, suddenly seemed cracked. I dismantled the mirror rig, recorked the mustard pots, and planted my brushes in a jar of turpentine. From the icebox I obtained a bottle of Riesling (evidently Conrad had arranged for my larder to remain stocked), then poured and consumed a glass.

I collapsed on the divan.

I slept, dreaming of spiders and infinities and fearful symmetries.

Shortly after midnight I awoke. She stood over me, her vermilion hair cascading down her bare shoulders, her satin gown cradled in her arms.

“It’s beautiful,” she said.

“Your portrait?”

“That, too, but I meant the gown. The pain is gone from my stomach. Death is a condition I could learn to abide. Why did you flip my face?”

“I had to use a mirror.”

“Of course.”

She dropped to her knees and kissed me fully on the lips.

“Can two Farbenmenschen do this?” I asked.

“I don’t know.”

Again she kissed me.

“It’s a distinct possibility,” I said.

Thus it happened that, one soft April night in 1915, in a makeshift atelier on the ground floor of an insane asylum, and despite the couple’s lamentable ontological status, Eros was appeased, passions were spent, and love knew its hour.

The following morning, shortly before noon, someone rapped four times on my door. H is for heaven, hell, hope, horror. I threw on a bathrobe. Ilona, dressed in a muslin chemise, followed me into the foyer.

"Fräulein, it's marvelous to see you," said Werner, addressing Ilona as he and Conrad stepped over the threshold. "Is your pain . . . ?"

"It's gone. But then again, so is Ilona Wessels of Holstenwall. Francis made a satin gown for her Farbenmensch self."

"Face, hair, gown—I knew his brush was equal to the challenge," said Conrad. "You've never looked more sublime."

"Sooner rather than later, we must review the dreadful events of Easter," said Ilona.

"Dear friends, I bring an invitation from Caligari," said Conrad. "He wants us all to have coffee in his office at four o'clock."

"A month ago, Ilona and I granted him such a request," I said, "and the results were disastrous."

"There will be no janissaries in the room," said Conrad. "I'm to brew and serve the coffee. He surrendered his pistol to me. He says he has momentous news."

"I'm amenable to visiting Herr Direktor, but right now I must ask you both a favor," said Ilona. "Francis's sitting room still contains a cabinet holding certain distasteful *memento mori*. Please arrange for its incineration."

"I understand," said Werner, retreating into the corridor.

"I simply don't want them around," said Ilona.

"I'll put our Grandmaster and his friends on the job."

"It's April," said Conrad, joining Werner in the corridor. "The furnace is dormant."

"There's turpentine in my classroom," I said.

Two hours later, the students appeared at my door. Saying not a word, they marched down the hallway and into the sitting room. Gaston grasped the narrow end of the cabinet. The paranoid and the space traveler lifted the bottom.

"After today, you'll never see us again," Ilona told them.

"I always liked your spiders, Ilona," said Pietro. "You were an excellent teacher, Mr. Wyndham."

"Next stop, Andromeda," said Commander Ruttluff of Die Erste Galaxisbrigade.

"Move twenty-eight: White slides a pawn to queen four," said Gaston. "Black deploys a bishop to king six—and then White resigns."

"With your permission, Mr. Wyndham," said Ludwig, "I'd like to hang these portraits of you and Ilona in our classroom."

"Of course," I said.

"But not just yet," said Ilona.

Later that afternoon my friends and I subjected ourselves to the typically distressing though never boring presence of Alessandro Caligari. The capitalist mystic was seated on the burgundy sofa, his hands resting on his perpendicular cane, peering at us from behind his black-rimmed spectacles. Werner, Ilona, and I slid into leather chairs before the teakwood table. She now wore her vermilion gown. Conrad, as promised, poured the coffee.

"Fräulein, I must confess I was quite moved by your *Totentanz*," said Caligari.

"Though not moved enough to spare it," noted Ilona.

"There is no percentage in pacifism, and yet antiwar sentiments will always enjoy a certain moral cachet," said Caligari, sipping coffee. "I wanted you four to be the first to know I've resolved to stop filling soldiers' minds with Kriegslust. There will be no sequel to *Verzückte Weisheit*."

"So what's next on your agenda?" said Ilona. "Bombing kindergartens?"

"From now on my energies will go exclusively into helping mental patients. Leutnant Slevoght, if you wish to once again practice art therapy here at Träumenchen, the position is yours."

"The greater the distance I can place between you and myself, Signore, the better," said Werner.

"Herr Röhrig, you may continue as my secretary for as long as you wish."

"Who can tell me the smallest unit of time?" said Conrad.

"My father could have," said Ilona.

"In any event, Conrad and I are moving to Berlin," said Werner. "We plan to open an art academy after the war ends."

"If you change your mind and paint another obscene picture," I told Caligari, "I'll destroy it just as I did *Ecstatic Wisdom*."

"No, you won't. You're living on borrowed time. 'Living' isn't quite the right word, is it, Mr. Wyndham?"

Ilona said, "So Herr Doktor finally got sick of all the blood on his hands . . ."

"I was a war profiteer, not a war criminal," said Caligari.

"Is there a difference?" said Werner.

"To my mind, yes. Alas, the generals and the princes don't need me anymore. They probably never needed me. Simple appeals to glory, God, and xenophobia would surely have delivered eager regiments into their hands. Please don't tell my customers that, or they'll want their gold back." Cesare pranced into the room and jumped into Caligari's lap. The alienist set down his porcelain cup and stroked the cat. "Occasionally, when he's on his game, a magician sees the world with great clarity. I'm sure you've had that experience, Fräulein."

"Not really, no," said Ilona.

"There are doors within doors, wheels within wheels, maps within maps," said Caligari. "Germany is a state, France is a state, Britain, Russia, Austria-Hungary, and—poised to enter the war next month on the side of the Entente—my native Kingdom of Italy. But beneath those states lies a deeper state, the invisible continent of expediency, beloved of kings, clerics, commissars, and capitalists, who can always depend on it to pile up whatever dead bodies need piling up, and the whole remorseless machine keeps functioning regardless of whatever paintings anybody hangs in a fucking museum."

Borrowed time. Indeed. I could hear the portals of eternity opening, their hinges creaking in my ear.

I glanced at Ilona. She heard them, too.

"Not only am I something of a Cagliostro, I am also a Nostradamus," said the alienist. "Would you like to know what's to come in this transcendently meaningless war? Shall I tell you about the horrors of Verdun? With good reason it will be called the meatgrinder. The bloodletting scheduled to occur along the River Somme? Over a million casualties. Shall we call them Sommenambulists? Eventually Britain will start producing self-propelled pillboxes like that contraption you brought here on Sunday. Despite many mechanical problems, they'll contribute prodigiously to the slaughter."

Ilona rested her cup on the table and stood up. "White resigns," she said, sidling away from her chair.

"Black resigns." I rose and followed Ilona as she headed toward the door.

"*Vita brevis, ars longa*," said Werner, gaining his feet.

"Late in 1918 an armistice will occur, and everyone will spend the next several years drafting and signing treaties," said Caligari, his voice sliding up and down in piercing glissandos, "until at long last the architects of the Great War can look back on their many accomplishments: a devastated France, a demoralized Britain, a ransacked

Belgium, a ruined Germany, a receiving line of corpses stretching from Armentières to Zanzibar!"

"I'm pleased to hear you're setting down your brush," Werner told Caligari. "You might be a competent sorcerer"—he marched across the salon—"but you've sullied enough canvases with your ersatz Expressionism."

"I cannot bring myself to say, 'Fare thee well, Alessandro,' but neither do I wish you ill," Conrad informed Caligari before joining the rest of us in the doorway. "Keep treating your patients through hypnotism and heteropathy and whatever else seems to work, and God may forgive you yet."

"The annexation of Weizenstaat by Luxembourg in compensation for the German occupation!" Caligari persisted, using his cane to lever himself off the divan. The cat vaulted from his lap and landed on the table. "The delivery of Russia into the hands of ideologically deluded fanatics! The ascent of mindless nationalism and virulent anti-Semitism following the fall of the Austro-Hungarian Empire! The creation of an artificially sectioned and perpetually chaotic Near East following the fall of the Ottoman Empire!"

Before escaping from Herr Direktor's domain, I glanced over my shoulder in time to see him raise his arm high and roil the air with his cane.

"And then, finally, planted in the soil of a distracted Europe and cultivated by professional psychopaths, the seeds of a second worldwide conflagration, destined to surpass the carnage quotient established by the first!"

As our sorrowful quartet descended to the grand lobby, I found myself taking a certain cold comfort in knowing that the prototype Francis Wyndham, the person of whom I was a mere aesthetic replica, was in no way privy to my present unenviable circumstances. Between his inert nothingness and my absurd somethingness lay only a welter of broken connections—fallen bridges, collapsed trestles, flooded roads, garbled syntax. It was a long, long way to Tipperary.

Upon reaching my bedroom, Ilona and I opened the closet and removed our two favorite exemplars of the Wessels-Wyndham theory of nonpictorial art. My particular effort, *Principia Insaniam*, suggested to me an ineffable but sensual encounter between a polyhedron and a tesseract. Ilona's canvas, *Serenade No. 6*, evoked foam dancing atop a love potion so powerful it could reconcile the universe to itself.

Clutching our canvases, we proceeded to the sitting room, where Werner and Conrad awaited us. Ilona's portrait of Francis Wyndham was still tilted against the casement. My portrait of her yet graced the easel. We laid our experiments in abstraction on the worktable.

"These are astonishing," said Werner, his palms hovering above the canvases as if to bless them.

"What are they supposed to *be*?" asked Conrad.

"They're supposed to be *being*," said Ilona.

"Of course," said Conrad, scowling.

"I dare say, Ilona has founded a new school of art," I said.

"Do you intend to take them with you?" asked Werner.

"Where we're going, pleasure is unknown," said Ilona, shaking her head. She pointed to *Serenade No. 6*. "Consider this my gift to you, Herr Slevoght."

"And *Principia Insanium* is my gift to you," I told Conrad.

"Both paintings will enter the curriculum of the Slevoght-Röhrig Academy of Fine Arts," said Werner. "Goodbye, Fräulein." He kissed Ilona on the brow, then turned to me and squeezed my shoulder. " 'And there's a law that things crawl off in the manner of snakes,' " he recited, " 'prophetically, dreaming on the hills of heaven.' "

Saying nothing, Conrad gave Ilona, then myself, a bony embrace.

I stroked Ilona's bounteous hair. She kissed me, then stepped through her portrait and vanished. I closed my eyes, heaved a sigh, and, pressing my face against the other canvas . . .

Entered the Farbenmenschen realm once more. I took Ilona's hand, though I couldn't feel her skin. Limned by an incandescent sunset, the fogbound bridge stretched to an unreachable horizon.

Ambling slowly forward, arm in arm, we passed other figures, but their beauty was lost on us, apprehension without appreciation. A girl with a pearl earring. A seated boy pulling a thorn from his foot. A sinewy young warrior balancing a sling on his shoulder. A sword-wielding woman and her maidservant absconding with a Babylonian general's head. A French postman with a forked beard. An aristocratic lady cradling a white weasel. A sorority of Post-Impressionist bathers. A cluster of Cubist *demoiselles* from Avignon. A nude descending a staircase.

As we continued our journey, Ilona and I grew benumbed by the knowledge that this endless span would never bring us anything beyond a melancholy procession of exquisite ghosts.

"*Vita brevis, pons longa*," I said. "Life is short, but the bridge is forever."

"White resigns," said Ilona.

"Black resigns," I said.

"White resigns, *ad infinitum*."

"Black does the same."

And yet, after a while, we agreed that eternity was a cut above oblivion. There was no hellfire in this place, nor hunger. We decided to remain. Call us obstinate shadows, insensate phantoms, angels without expectations. Call us the children of the bridge. We are walking there still.

# ABOUT THE AUTHOR

Having arrived on the planet in 1947, James Morrow spent his adolescence in Hillside Cemetery, not far from his birthplace in Philadelphia, pursuing his passion for 8mm genre moviemaking. Before going off to college, he and his friends used their favorite graveyard location for a half dozen fantasy and horror films, including adaptations of "The Rime of the Ancient Mariner" and "The Tell-Tale Heart."

After receiving degrees from the University of Pennsylvania and Harvard University, Morrow redirected his storytelling energies toward the production of satiric novels and stories. His acerbic assessment of the nuclear arms race, *This Is the Way the World Ends*, was a Nebula Award finalist and the BBC's selection as best SF novel of 1986. His next dark comedy, *Only Begotten Daughter*, chronicling the escapades of Jesus's divine half-sister in contemporary Atlantic City, won the World Fantasy Award and the animosity of theocrats everywhere.

Throughout the 1990s, Morrow devoted his energies to killing God, an endeavor he pursued through three interconnected novels: *Towing Jehovah* (World Fantasy Award), *Blameless in Abaddon* (*New York Times* Notable Book), and *The Eternal Footman* (Grand Prix de l'Imaginaire finalist). Having grown sick of his Creator, and vice-versa, the author next attempted to dramatize the birth of the scientific worldview. Critic Janet Maslin called *The Last Witchfinder* "provocative book-club bait" and "an inventive feat." A thematic sequel, *The Philosopher's Apprentice*, was praised by NPR as "an ingenious riff on Frankenstein." Morrow's most recent irreverent epic, *Galápagos Regained*, narrates the adventures of Charles Darwin's fictional zookeeper.

The author's acclaimed cycle of stand-alone novellas includes *City of Truth* (Nebula Award), *Shambling Towards Hiroshima* (Theodore Sturgeon Memorial Award), and *The Madonna and the Starship*. Morrow's work has been translated into thirteen languages. He lives in State College, Pennsylvania, with his wife, Kathryn, and two enigmatic dogs.